MW01076360

Dramatic Literacy

USING DRAMA AND LITERATURE
TO TEACH
MIDDLE-LEVEL CONTENT

J. Lea Smith • *J. Daniel Herring*

HEINEMANN
Portsmouth, NH

Heinemann
A division of Reed Elsevier Inc.
361 Hanover Street
Portsmouth, NH 03801–3912
www.heinemann.com

Offices and agents throughout the world

Library of Congress Cataloging-in-Publication Data
Smith, J. Lea.
    Dramatic literacy : using drama and literature to teach middle-level content /
J. Lea Smith, J. Daniel Herring.
        p. cm.
    Includes bibliographical references.
    ISBN 0-325-00050-6
    1. Drama in education.   I. Herring, J. Daniel.   II. Title.

PN3171 .S635   2001
373.139′9 — dc21

00-054167

Editor: Lisa A. Barnett
Production: Abigail M. Heim
Cover design: Jenny Jensen Greenleaf/Greenleaf Illustration and Design
Manufacturing: Steve Bernier

Printed in the United States of America on acid-free paper
05   04   03   02   01   VP   1   2   3   4   5

To our parents for their unconditional love and support

Leah L. Smith
Mary Elsie and Kenneth L. Mitchell
Thomas N. and Verna B. Herring

And to the memory of Alpha Omega, whose stories made us laugh on the days when laughter was the recipe for inspiration.

Contents

Acknowledgments

We need to thank many people for various reasons. We would like to express our acknowledgments jointly and separately.

First, we thank our editor Lisa A. Barnett for keeping the faith and knowing we would bring *Dramatic Literacy* to life. We are indebted to Ben and Jean Matthews, who graciously provided a secluded location in their guesthouse so that the final chapters of this book could be completed. We give thanks to God for the spiritual guidance needed on a daily basis. Much gratitude goes to the many students and colleagues who told us they wanted our dramatic-literature approach in a book and who allowed us to use their classrooms as a place of exploration and discovery. And most importantly we thank the children who inspire us to teach.

To Vincent, a little boy in my long-ago first grade classroom, I thank you, wherever you are, for showing me how literature and drama fit together as a way to learn and to teach. I wish to acknowledge Lewis B. Smith, Stanley Mour, Nel Noddings, and George Spindler for encouraging me to try the unknown. They, along with others, have played a significant role in my professional life. I thank Martin Schmidt for knowing when to help a struggling artist. I thank mi familia Plancarte plus my brother James and my sister Marilyn. Stacey Vanek Smith and Kandice L. Knigge never ceased to ask about *Dramatic Literacy*. Thanks to my friends, students, and colleagues for conversations, for listening, and for caring. I give thanks to each person I have met along life's roadway for each has enriched my journey. I am thankful my path intersected with J. Daniel Herring, my coauthor. (JL)

First and foremost, I thank Roger L. Bedard for introducing me to the field of Drama and Theatre for Youth. For providing the solid foundation on which I began to walk my career path, I give much gratitude to Lin Wright, Don Doyle, and Johnny Saldana. Developing as an artist is tough, and I thank Maureen Shea and David Saar for the beginnings of that journey, and Moses Goldberg for his never-ending commitment to my growth. For their love and friendship, without which I cannot imagine my life, I thank Katie Blackerby, Beth Conn, Steven Jones (and Justin), Gabriel Morrow, Raymond Nuesch, Patricia Squires Seitz, Mary Beth vanderHoek (Alex and Marcus, too), and last but certainly not least my coauthor, J. Lea Smith. (JD)

Foreword

Language researchers (Halliday, 1979–80; Luke and Freebody, 1997) would say that process drama puts its emphasis on *learning language* (comprehension and interpretation), *learning about language* (perspective, voice, aesthetics), *learning through language* (inquiry), and *learning to use language to critique* (critical literacy). Since the function of a foreword is to provide perspective, I want to use this framework to situate J. Lea Smith and J. Daniel Herring's book, *Dramatic Literacy: Using Drama and Literature to Teach Middle-Level Content.*

When I told the first graders at the Center for Inquiry in Indianapolis that I was writing the foreword to a book on drama and I wanted to hear from them as to what I should say, their response was, "Tell 'em that it's fun!" While that response may not strike you as profound, to my way of thinking, it's almost reason enough in itself to advocate the use of drama in schools.

I'm convinced that drama is one of the reasons that the children in the Center scored so well on our state's standardized test of educational progress. Last year our inner-city, largely African American students (a group historically not well served by either schools or testing) outperformed the first rung of suburban schools making up greater Indianapolis (Leland, 1999). They not only read a lot, but they had fun.

Raymond Williams (1977) says that any "definition of language is always, implicitly or explicitly, a definition of human beings in the world." What Williams says of language is what Smith and Herring say of drama.

Because literacy is fundamentally about learning to use language to *mean*, drama and good books go together. What is a reading program, or education for that matter, without stories into which you can sink your teeth? Many educators fail to make the connection between quality literature and quality reading programs. If there is nothing new to learn in what is being read, there is little or no motivation for children to engage in the process. One of the first things that will delight readers of *Dramatic Literacy,* then, is the number of good books with which they will become familiar as well as the repertoire of strategies they can use to bring these books to life for children. There is everything here from techniques to units of study; ideas for the timid teacher of drama as well as for the gutsy.

People who know me know that I advocate inquiry-based education. In inquiry-based education, the focus is on the underlying process of inquiry—observation, conversation, transmediation (e.g., recasting your understanding of a story into art or drama), attending to tension, reflection, critique, and the taking of new action. Both drama and inquiry-based education see curriculum in terms of learning. The authors of *Dramatic Literacy* argue that drama represents "a natural approach to learning" and therefore, in addition to the reading and language arts curriculum, they have included chapters about the use of drama in social science, science, and mathematics.

My latest interest is critical literacy. I want to argue that to be truly literate, children have to understand the socially constructed nature of literacy. They need to understand that how they view things is not how everyone views things. Their experiences and home cultures have constructed them as particular kinds of literate beings; beings who value some things and marginalize other things, including abilities and peoples. Interrogating the dominant culture and the systems of meaning that operate is difficult, but drama helps.

At one point in this volume, J. Lea Smith and J. Daniel Herring argue that in drama we invite children to "be characters, not do caricatures." Because knowledge is dynamic, reflective, and critical, students of all ages need to live the curriculum firsthand, including understanding and critiquing the social practices that lead them, when questioned, to say, "Why? Because that's just the kind of person I am." Drama helps learners understand that common sense is always someone's cultural sense, and that without this awareness they will continue, like others in their society, to have their hands in the cookie jar.

Dramatic Literacy poses *drama as curriculum* rather than drama in the service of curriculum. This is drama being highly literate and literacy being entirely dramatic. I know that *Dramatic Literacy* will become a staple in the Teaching to Learn / Learning to Teach teacher education program we run at the Center for Inquiry in Indianapolis. I also know that we will have fun using it.

Jerome C. Harste
Indiana University, Bloomington

Halliday, M. A. K. 1979–80. "Three Aspects of Children's Language Development: Learning Language, Learning through Language, Learning about Language." In *Oral and Written Language Development Research: Impact on the Schools*. Edited by Y. Goodman, M. Haussler, and D. Strickland. Urbana, IL: National Council of Teachers of English, 7–19.

Leland, C. 1999. *Exemplary Reading Programs*. Newark, DE: International Reading Association.

Luke, Allan, and Peter Freebody. 1997. "Shaping the Social Practices of Reading." In *Constructing Critical Literacies*. Edited by Sandy Muspratt, Allan Luke, and Peter Freebody. Cresskill, NJ: Hampton Press, 185–225.

Williams, Raymond. 1977. *Marxism and Literature*. Oxford: Oxford University Press.

Foreword

"More human beings than ever before see more drama than ever before and are more directly influenced, conditioned, programmed by drama than ever before. Drama has become one of the principal vehicles of information, one of the prevailing methods of 'thinking' about life and its situations."

MARTIN ESSLIN, 1987

Young people are surrounded by drama. They crave ways to express themselves—and drama is an ideal medium for that expression. Of course they must be literate in this art form. They must understand and appreciate both how it is formed and performed and the meanings it creates. They should be able to express themselves through drama, the art form that naturally grows out of their youthful pretend play. They should be able to construct their own meanings in their performances as a way to make sense of their world. Improvisation, a controlled continuation of youthful play, is the natural, active way for young people to become literate in drama.

Helping young people become deeply involved in their own improvisations can be a very enjoyable process. Having a solid foundation in the discipline of drama and a collection of sound strategies for the classroom will lead to success for teacher and student. *Dramatic Literacy* is an outstanding text designed to do just that.

Chapter 1, with well-documented research support, explains the varied roles of drama in the classroom. This insight is important to assure that the drama makes best use of students' valuable time. The purpose of the work should be clear to both student and teacher. The drama should never be just "putting on a skit"; it should be involvement in the art form as a way to make meaning.

Chapter 2, "Drama's ABCs," explains the essentials of the art form—character, conflict, and setting—the *who*, the *what*, and the *where* that form the building blocks of the scenes to be enacted. The art form is honored, as it should be. Here, too, is an explanation of two basic strategies the teacher can use as a means to draw the students into the drama—*side-coaching* and *stepping into role*.

Chapter 3 outlines two major methodologies for structuring the dramatic experience rarely found in a single text. One, the linear approach, is developed out of U.S. teaching used to dramatize a story. The other, holistic drama, is developed from British work created to "drop students into a role at the 'gut level,' (Wagner, 1976) without instruction in dramatic skills." There are a number of differences in the preparation and role of the teacher for each methodology. As the text points out, "the middle-level teacher initiating drama into his classroom for the first time may prefer the linear structure . . . [since] the drama activities are primarily planned and outlined by the teacher before involving the students in the dramatic play [thus giving] the teacher greater control." In contrast, the teacher using the holistic approach must be prepared to make more decisions during the drama session itself. Familiarity with each method will make the drama work much richer for both teacher and student.

The remainder of the text is devoted to practical examples of approaches to dramatizing a story and to using drama as a part of language arts, social studies, science, math, and second language instruction. The examples are soundly presented with objectives or focus questions organizing each lesson, a clear description of the classroom planning/playing or process/procedure, and suggestions for a final evaluation of the dramatic work. Students involved in these lessons will be able to do what the national theater standards outline as essential for dramatic literacy.

The primary strength of this text is its sound interweaving of theory and practice. An understanding both of the art form and of the learning process is essential to making classroom drama of real value to the students. The in-text lesson plans can act as a springboard to creating new lessons. Implementing the text lessons combined with the theory can give each teacher the skills to create her own plans designed to meet the specific needs of her classes.

Another strength of this text is the student audience addressed—youth in the middle school. Many of the texts in our field are written for younger children or are theater books for the high school theater student. Here is a very usable text for the energetic, challenging pre- and early teen. The work is solid and the basics will be useful for students of all ages.

Use and enjoy!

Lin Wright
Arizona State University

Esslin, Martin. 1987. *The Field of Drama: How the Signs of Drama Create Meaning on Stage and Screen.* London: Methuen.

Introduction

Just how did a children's literature professor and a professional theater director join forces to work in classrooms using books and drama as a way to teach and learn? We met at the Kentucky Institute for Arts in Education during the summer of 1989. And from there we began talking of how we might bring together literature and drama. We had long conversations over dinner and we also had sticky discussions as to how we might be able to create an instructional curriculum built on literature and drama.

One of our first endeavors together with drama and literature was in a primary classroom. Our purpose was to explore the possibilities of how we might weave together reading a good book and then showing, through drama, students' interpretation of the characters, plot, and setting. J. Daniel led K–1 children through a variety of dramatic activities as J. Lea videotaped. We then would review the tapes and study what appeared to work and how we might wish to adapt our methods to use drama-literature as a learning process at all grade levels.

We put time, thought, and considerable energy into working through how we then could begin to show teachers, students, and colleagues the tremendous instructional possibilities a literature-drama approach has in a teaching setting. Naturally, we have grown as drama-literature teachers as we have worked with the concept of demonstrating learning through reading, writing, and dramatic action. One of our greatest joys was playing with all of the ins and outs of integrating literature-drama into content teaching. We attempt, in *Dramatic Literacy,* to portray our learning.

Drama is examined as a learning modality to build on a constructivist approach to learning. In a constructivist learning environment, students discover and construct meaning from prior experiences as they interact with new experiences. They process information by analyzing data to detect patterns, forming and testing hypotheses, and integrating the new knowledge within their prior experience (Elkind, 1979; Piaget, 1969; Siegel, 1984; Vygostsky, 1978). Learning is an active, constructive process of playing with ideas, concepts, and perceptions.

Drama is a mode for learning and responding. Drama creates a setting where a person is able to explore and experiment with content through self-perception, social interaction, movement, and language—reading, writing, speaking, and listening. Integrating drama into content studies provides the middle-level learner with a learning environment which supports their developmental needs for voice and ownership in the learning process.

The basics teachers need to know as they begin to work with drama as instruction are simple—drama is a way of learning through role playing and problem solving. It is a creative way of using the whole body to transmit and receive information with mind, body, and voice working in collaboration to create a total picture. To facilitate a drama session, a teacher 1) creates appropriate dramatic action, 2) facilitates individual and group involvement in the drama, and 3) guides individuals within the group toward understanding the drama created.

One way of initiating drama in middle-level studies is through the use of a linear approach (Ward, 1957). This structure is primarily planned and outlined by the teacher prior to involving the students in the dramatic playing. The linear drama session resembles a recipe. The steps include: 1) planning; 2) playing; and 3) evaluating. In contrast the basic holistic method gets students to drop into a role at the gut level, (Wagner, 1976) without dramatic skills instruction. Students are encouraged to live the invented life (of the drama) in an improvisational framework. In a holistic session students assume the attitudes of a character, have external actions symbolize internal meaning, and develop an understanding of the themes, values, and issues of the material enacted (Wright and Herring, 1987).

Life is a story. And because stories communicate life's realities, they play an important role in studying and understanding all dimensions of the human experience. The stories in children's literature portray the human experience and examine the primal issues of existence. Literature allows a young reader to look into other lives, while it gives those lives shape and embeds them in a culture (Applebee, 1991; Levstick, 1992).

Our students spend a part of each day in a classroom studying content that may seem unrelated and unconnected to the stories in their lives. If we want students to connect with these stories of life, we might begin by integrating children's literature into content studies through dramatization. Literature dramatizations then become the lens through which the content is viewed. This lens holds the learner's attention while connecting content with the variety of human experiences.

Effectively teaching the language arts in a middle-level setting requires teachers to create stimulating, language-rich environments that provide students with genuine and meaningful purposes for using language. In a process language arts classroom, students operate in a workshop setting where they build speaking, listening, writing, and reading fluency on self-choice, ownership, and purposeful involvement in the learning cycle. Drama is a natural fit with a process language arts curriculum based on students' interpretation of their reality.

Social studies is a reflection of the moral, social, and economical context of our past, present, and future. Yet, even when teachers present such a valid argument to students, students still fail to note the relevance of social studies to their present and future lives. Perhaps this argument is part of the problem of teaching and learning social studies. We need to start viewing social studies from a more personal and current perspective. Social studies is more than a product, it is a process of understanding and clarifying the continuum of human motives as they relate to individuals as well as societies and cultures at large. "Drama is human beings confronted by situations which change them because of what they must face in dealing with those challenges" (Heathcote, 1984, 48). Drama instructional activities can connect to the social studies curriculum to create a learning setting where students are able to try-on social experiences, explore the diversity of the global world, or walk in the shoes of a historical figure.

The major goal in science education is to develop people who can think critically about scientific phenomena. The processes of science enable students to explore the world and make educated guesses. Facts alone are not sufficient for our technological world. And learning science process skills solely from reading textbooks is like trying to learn to ride a bike from an instructional manual. The process skills in science involve: observing, comparing, classifying, measuring, communicating, inferring, predicting, hypothesizing, and defining and controlling variables to interpret data. These same skills are components of drama. Scientific concepts will be more likely learned and retained by students if presented in a variety of ways and extended over a period of time. Drama and science together can provide the middle-level learner with a way to explore, experiment, and interpret the science all around us each day.

Growth and learning in mathematics can be enhanced in an atmosphere of inquiry, investigation, analysis of mathematical situations, and problem solving. It is through such an atmosphere that students are actively engaged in the construction of ideas. And it is this active view of learning that links mathematics and drama. Drama is a natural strategy to build a learning environment where students are constructing their understanding of mathematics. Incorporating the processes of drama creates situations where students are staging mathematical concepts through group or individual presentations. In addition, students have a concrete example or experience to base their mathematics concept construction. This real experience also encourages students to talk and write about their thinking and discuss with others what they are doing as they do it.

The linguistic and social knowledge necessary for meaningful human-to-human communication builds on "knowing how, when, and what to say what to whom" (Standards for Foreign Language Learning, 1993). Traditionally, second language instruction was built on a study of grammar and vocabulary. Today, the Coalition of Foreign Language Organizations (1993) encourages a more hands-on approach where the learning of a second language is the ability to communicate in meaningful and appropriate ways with users of other languages. The prevailing principle to guide second language curriculum development is communication, where the why, the whom, and the when form the content to design purposeful instructional episodes.

Drama isn't just an add-on to middle-level classroom instruction. Drama doesn't have to happen only when the specialist is invited to the classroom. Drama can and should become a must in daily instructional activities for each content area.

When students are engaged in learning through drama they find ownership, challenge, and voice in the content under study. Drama is a learning process that eliminates students' passivity and fosters individual as well as cooperative learning. This student-centered approach builds on and meets the student's developmental needs. Drama can form the basis of a student-centered curriculum where students are able to demonstrate what they know. The dramatic process requires the learner to perform, write, discuss, listen, problem-solve, reflect on thinking, critically think, interact with others, create, build relationships, play, have fun, yet be powerfully engaged with their study of content.

Our one wish for you is that you experiment with drama-literature in your classroom. Our book shares our classroom experiences. We try to highlight clearly key points to support your initial efforts to be more successful. You will meet first-hand the power of literature-drama as a way to teach and, if you are willing to take the plunge and integrate literacy and dramatic action into content instruction. Our lessons are just a beginning.

J. Lea Smith and J. Daniel Herring

1

Drama: A Natural Approach to Learning

"As we work to improve the quality of education for all children, the arts must be recognized as a vital part of our effort."

RICHARD RILEY, 1993
SECRETARY OF EDUCATION

Focus Question   **What role can drama play in middle-level instruction?**

A Close-Up of Drama

I was faced by another obstacle, turning over in bed, or letting the nurses turn me. Talk about fear and pain, my ribs squiggling around inside me, my reward for turning: My mother with an ice cold ginger ale. I sucked up all the pain inside me, closed my eyes tight, and held my bear. I turned.

I also had to learn to use my arms and legs. . . . Physical therapists came to me every day, moving legs and arms, helping me to remember what moving my limbs felt like. I was weak, yet the day for me to stand came quick. My legs warbled, my feet still numb, it was as if I had never stood before, it was all new. Before I knew it, more days passed and it was time to walk. I forgot how to walk, I had to relearn. I would lean on my mother's back, and my therapist would move my legs. I wanted to walk so bad, I could not give up, I made my self stand, I made my self do it, I made my self walk. I relearned how to walk. I overcame an obstacle most people encounter once in their life, twice. I learned to walk, stand, and use my arms and legs again.

This went on for about two months, and eventually I got the hang of walking. I could do it again, like an ole' pro. I was strong, I was almost back to normal. I could lift books, roll over, you know what, I could even tie my shoe. Nothing stood in my way then, and I know that nothing can ever stand in my way, I can conquer anything.

Joanna Gohmann, July 2000

Looking closely, we see a teacher use drama—personal monologue—to create a learning environment where a study of content merges language fluency, social development, and self-awareness. This classroom vignette reveals drama as a powerful and natural context to support the middle-level learner. Students wrote, read, listened, and performed through speaking a personal experience. While engaged in social interaction, students were able to relate concretely to the reality that each of us sees with our own eyes.

Drama and the Learner

In our middle-level instruction, we meet a number of students who seem uninterested in learning. Their attitude suggests they believe that school is unwilling and unable to meet their interests or concerns. As teachers, we often are put off by this apathetic behavior and push them to study. Stepping back, we have discovered that we may fail our learners by not providing a means for direct involvement in the learning cycle.

A student is undergoing changes that involve a dynamic interplay between self-identity, social interaction, and cognitive development. And if we fail to recognize this change, we will miss the opportunity to support the learning of our students.

Our instructional design needs to take into account the evolving nature of each learner as they struggle with self-identity, explore the dimensions of social interaction, and extend their creative and critical thinking skills.

As we struggled to modify our instruction we tried several different strategies that would build on the uniqueness of our learners. Our students come to us from a diverse cultural heritage coupled with a vast array of experiences and ideas about the world. Our instruction must meet and address their individual viewpoints through a variety of approaches. Learners need to be able to talk, move, and make choices as they interact with content, and as members of a community of learners feel safe enough to share their individual ideas. Integrating drama into the middle-level instructional curriculum is a means to meet a learner's need for multiple means to respond.

Drama as a Learning Modality

We know that learning is an active, constructive process of coming to know. Understanding is a building process that changes perspective through reflection and interaction with others (Short & Burke, 1991). Through our classroom involvement with learners, we have found that drama can provide a process to learn, by living through or experiencing. Drama is a potentially powerful tool for making connections among learning, content, and students.

Drama provides a learning modality especially well suited for cultivating thinking dispositions. Perkins (1994) refers to a disposition as a felt tendency, commitment, and enthusiasm. Dispositions more than strategies may be the key to helping learners mobilize their mental powers as well as their interest. For instance, when the instructional strategy calls for a discussion of a story's plot sequence, students are encouraged to demonstrate their knowledge of plot through dramatization. This instructional disposition builds on the student's natural developmental characteristics of verbal interaction as well as using a different learning modality—physical movement to demonstrate understanding. The dramatic interpretation of the story provides the students with the opportunity to play the cause and effects of the story's plot, permitting them to view the outcome from multiple vantage points and thus nurture open-ended thinking.

Encounters with drama are never end-points; they challenge us to new experiences. A "route" as Merleau-Ponty described, is "an experience which gradually clarifies itself, which gradually rectifies itself and proceeds by dialogue with itself and with others" (1964, p. 21). The relevance of drama is to feel oneself en route, to feel oneself in a place where there are always possibilities. We, through drama and literature, can awaken students to their everyday situations, enable them to make sense, and to name their worlds (Greene, 1992). What drama provides the learner is the ability to ask and to examine what could happen next, what would have happened if this had occurred, or what is life like after this? A group of students studying *Tuck Everlasting* (Babbitt, 1975) were asked to portray an incident in their own life as it is now, as it will be in 50 years, and in a 100 years. The impetus of this dramatic episode was to examine what it would be like to live forever and what society may resemble as a way of looking at possibilities. And perhaps it is this factor alone that enables drama to be a powerful tool to use with middle-level students.

Drama is a way of learning through role playing and problem solving. This process of learning through drama calls for self-awareness, communication skills, concentration, and group cooperation. It is an imaginative way to use the whole person to transmit and receive information with mind, body, and voice working in collaboration to create a total picture. Drama is a means to be resourceful, to see what could be as well as what is. And drama requires a different kind of sensitivity, or intelligence. Highlighted in drama is an incisive ability to size up very quickly what is going on in a situation (Gardner, 1985). This capacity is a natural dimension of communicating.

Recently a science class was examining the issues of health reform. To enable students to address problems surrounding this issue, we elected to use a role-playing activity that involved them as professional hospital staff, persons needing immediate medical care, or insurance company staff. This process began with these three groups debating what universal coverage should include (e.g., heart transplants, broken bones, plastic surgery) and went on to address moral questions concerning who should receive coverage with limited funds. This dramatic learning process provided these students with the opportunity to take on the roles of communicator and problem solver while examining relevant issues in a situation that allowed for thoughtful reflection and learning. Drama enables learners to experience the concepts under study. It also provides learners with the opportunity to make choices, become actively engaged in learning experiences that are developmentally appropriate, and evaluate the learning process. Drama seems to create a more cooperative learning environment that provides for students to have a say in the learning activities. After a dramatization, students seem to be more willing to discuss topics from multiple perspectives while examining their own feelings. We notice that drama initiates an interaction between the learner and the content that sparks genuine learning by integrating what they experience into their system of understanding. Thus, drama is a natural and effective instructional tool when teachers are willing to share center stage with their students (Smith and Herring, 1994).

Drama as Language

Using drama as a mode of learning builds on one of the oldest forms of communication—physical action and oral interpretation. Thus drama combines nonverbal and verbal communication based on cognitive reasoning. Language is the vehicle by which thought is socialized and thus made logical, but it is not the original basis of, nor does it ever become the whole of, human thinking (Piaget, 1926). Piaget also points out that linguistic signs are not the first signifier of thought, but rather private symbols for which there are no signs. For example, the shaking of the legs may represent the movement of the fringe on a baby blanket, sucking the thumb may represent going to sleep, and the opening and closing of the mouth may represent the opening and closing of a toy box. Each of these events is an imitation. And it is when these imitations are internalized that they become images that are the first true signifiers of cognitive reasoning (Phillips, 1969). "The mind transforms perception, and mediates with the environment through acts" (Courtney, 1980, p. 38). And when we take the perceptions we receive and re-create them in the mind into imaginings, we then are able to express these in nonverbal and verbal dramatic acts.

Dramatic action then, is symbolic communication that provides a context for language development. Many recent educational publications maintain a significant relationship between drama and the acquisition of language skills, yet Bolton (1979) suggests that in many ways drama is language. " . . . drama is a cobweb and language its strands; you cannot conceive of one without the other" (p. 119).

Language development is therefore built upon prior physical and verbal experiential and social opportunities. Courtney (1980) argues that "learning to speak is built upon learning to act dramatically. But it is not merely that dramatic action is genetically earlier—it is assumed by the acts of speaking and writing. Dramatic action is the very foundation of language learning" (Courtney, 1980, p. 38).

In support of the interlink between drama and language development are Bruner's (1974) three stages of language growth: (1) the *enactive,* where the child can only know the world through performance; (2) the *iconic,* where images stand for events; and (3) the *symbolic,* where the meaning of the symbol becomes specific rather than general. Examining these language stages, we recognize that nonverbal thought as well as interaction between people becomes the basis of two-way communication, a dialogue. This process is where drama and language work in tandem to demonstrate cognition and interpretation.

As a child moves into adolescence, language and drama begin to operate on a more abstract level to represent thinking and interpretation. Thus the use of language and drama is not concretely tied to imitation to demonstrate meaning. Rather, the learner uses drama and language to give shape to other types of thinking through talking, listening, reading, and writing.

Drama becomes a matrix for continued language development and refinement. Moffett (1983) conceives of drama as the basis for the ideas and actions of language behaviors. Drama becomes a means to foster the learner's language ability to: (1) refine listening skills by actively engaging in dialogue; (2) invent specific speech to accomplish particular outcomes; (3) mold the language style, voice, and mannerisms of a dramatic persona; (4) switch roles in a given situation which encourages seeing multiple perspectives of self and others; (5) identify and understand the forces involved in a dramatic structure—reading, writing, and acting; and (6) express his or her real feelings in a safe, pretend environment. Building learning on drama enables the learner to engage in varying language activities that extend language competence and support the extension of self in addition to the acquisition of content.

One way to support a student's language refinement and content learning through drama is to engage the learner in both improvised and scripted drama as performer, writer, and respondent. A group of students studying Shakespeare's *Hamlet* could first read the play, next improvise a variety of scenes from the original text using modern-day language and setting, then write/script these new scenes complete with dialogue and monologue, and finally conclude the project with a class discussion on the themes found within both versions. The students now have processed language through written, verbal, and kinesthetic modalities, while building an instructional episode on drama. Thus drama becomes a pivotal mode of learning combining both nonverbal and verbal communication.

Drama as Self-Awareness

The process of defining oneself is a social one. Each new task and situation that a learner masters brings them closer to a set of cultural expectations of who they can be. In a paradoxical way, the achievements that bring one closer to an individual identity also tie one closer to a social group (Erikson, 1968).

Drama nurtures the student's sense of individuality, which helps to strengthen the cognitive structure of the self. The definition of self evolves from all of one's activities. This is particularly true when the learner is encouraged to examine self in a supportive context where they make deliberate decisions. Drama, by definition, is an intentional and self-determined process that should contribute to what a person defines as his or her being (Csikszentmihalyi and Schiefele, 1992).

During learning the search for a personal identity is one of critical significance. In this process, learners examine many of the philosophical, psychological, social, and physical options available to them. They then attempt to try out numerous self-images and behaviors, and either accept or reject them. Maslow (1971) suggests that belonging and esteem are crucial. However, as teachers we often overlook these needs as we push students to be more self-actualizing. To address these needs we can involve learners in dramatic projects that involve creating a script from improvised activities, building a set for a play, or participating in a series of drama sessions on a central theme or idea. These provide the setting to explore choice and self-direction. Through these projects, students acquire not only artistic skills, but also knowledge of what it means to complete a meaningful venture. This involvement initiates the evolving development of coming to know self while encouraging self-esteem. And learners have the opportunity to observe their own development and growth and personal contributions to a collaborative activity of some scope (Gardner, 1990).

When using drama at the middle level, students are able to experiment with different roles, behaviors, and attitudes as they move toward greater self-awareness which in turn fosters greater self-esteem. Self-esteem is a belief in one's own honest self, confidence in one's abilities, and the capacity to partici-pate actively whether alone or in group efforts. Through dramatic activities, students learn to depend on themselves by relying on their own visions and impulses. This allows them to take personal risks to interact and explore con-tent concepts with others. Respect for self and others is generally acquired through satisfying, enjoyable experiences in which an individual can gain confidence (Siks, 1983).

Drama as Social Development

Social development includes those actions that support learners to interact effectively with others (Jensen, Sloane, and Young, 1988). Erikson (1968) pro-poses that we form our identities within the context of social relationships. It is through social relationships that social competence, a critical dimension of maturing, is attempted. Most young people refine their social skills natu-rally; however, others may require assistance to develop and refine these skills in order to associate and communicate meaningfully with their world. Stu-dents operating at all levels of social competence contribute to the creation of a learning environment that forms and extends social skills development. Learners, at whatever level of social competence, need the opportunity to develop multilayered social skills through authentic and meaningful interac-tions with one another. All learners benefit from instruction built on social interaction.

Social interactions are a fundamental aspect of drama. Drama by its very nature involves students in social contexts where they are required to think, talk, manipulate concrete materials, and share viewpoints in order to arrive at decisions (Siks,1977). To use drama as an instructional process creates a so-cial learning structure where individuals form groups functioning as a whole. It is during this process of group interaction that students learn social skills in an authentic setting as they deal with each other as well as multiple perspec-tives and presentation. For drama to support social skills development, and for a genuine group process to occur, each student needs to contribute. For example, using drama as part of team-building instruction, we asked students individually to select an object in the room that would then become a part of a group-created still-life sculpture. After creating the group sculpture, students individually talked about why they chose their object. This sharing was followed by a group discussion of how they had created their sculpture. Later, this sculpture came to life through drama and creative movement. By using this social interaction—individual and group responses—the drama and creative movement activities supplied a learning environment where team-building augmented social development.

Heathcote (1984) believes that drama confronts students with situations that may change them because of what they must face in dealing with issues. Drama puts students into other people's shoes by using personal experience and factual knowledge to help them understand other points of view. These experiences allow students to put their feet into another's shoes, but once they begin to walk in those shoes, their response is generated from the other's perspective. During this exchange, they begin to feel, imagine, and create an experience that may be foreign. This exchange of perspectives encourages genuine social interaction as an individual is able to see how another feels, responds, reacts, and lives within a given situation (Heathcote cited in Johnson and O'Neill, 1984). It is then through drama that students are able to explore content concepts while trying on varying social experiences.

As we worked with a social studies class studying cultural prejudice, we recognized their need to try on a culture that is different from their own. In one drama session students were assigned to one of two hypothetical cultures in which they characterized the perspectives, behaviors, mannerisms, and ideals associated with the people of that culture. Students were encouraged to walk in the shoes of someone else. Yet to merge self-awareness, social experiences, and content, students would need to experience what it is like being an outsider. We arranged, as a component of the drama playing, for the two distinct cultures to meet and to socialize. Through role playing and follow-up discussion, this dramatic episode addressed issues surrounding cultural prejudices. Many of the students expressed an awareness of and willingness to consider differences not necessarily as a negative but rather as a uniqueness.

Drama is a natural approach to content instruction for middle-level students. By nature, our students are social, and as teachers we need to provide a meaningful avenue for them to use their energies and social needs to foster learning. Students want to be actively involved in learning activities and to be personally connected to the educational process (Smith and Johnson, 1993). Atwell (1987) encourages us to incorporate the realities of development into our instructional design. Drama is an ideal vehicle for reaching the wide spectrum of culturally and linguistically diverse students who are often skirting the fringes of more traditional instructional curriculum.

Drama as Instruction

Drama's powerful force lies in its potential to place learners in a variety of contexts—in situations that generate forms of thought, feeling, and language beyond those usually generated in traditional instructional settings (Edmiston, 1991). In addition, drama enhances ability in all other academic areas by making students better thinkers (Corathers, 1991). Thus drama gives a creative and psychological balance to more academic instruction.

Drama has considerable potential as a process for learning with significant implications within the school curriculum. It is an experience that supports the development of the following cognitive processes: questioning, critical and constructive thought, problem solving, comparison, interpretation, judgment, discrimination, and expanded learning and research (O'Neill and Lambert, 1985).

Mode of Presentation and Mode of Response

The major obstacles to students' learning are not primarily cognitive in nature (Csikszentmihalyi, 1990). The problem isn't that students cannot learn; rather it is that students don't want to learn. A typical approach to middle-level education is to develop better thinking through step-by-step procedures. However, the problem with this view is that the learner often finds such strategies artificial and unappealing, which results in boredom and a sense of futility. Helpful as this stepwise approach may be in a technical way, it fails to capture the learner's enthusiasm and commitment.

One of the least considered options in creating curriculum are the modalities through which students encounter and express what they learn (Eisner, 1985). We tend to limit our students to only a few forms of expression to learn content as well as demonstrate their grasp of the content. In most middle-level classrooms, students usually study a social studies lesson, a scientific phenomenon, or a novel by reading a textbook, writing a paper, or discussing it in class. Although the use of reading, writing, or discussion to instruct students is relevant, other forms of instruction remain wholly untapped. Educational instruction needs to provide learners with an awareness that understanding is secured and experienced in different ways. Instruction needs to be sculpted and responsive to the concept that individuals have quite different ways of learning and knowing from one another. Rather than ignoring individual differences or pretending they don't exist, we must guarantee our students an educational experience that maximizes their intellectual potential (Gardner, 1993).

In a classroom setting, students frequently are asked to demonstrate what they know in a particular content area through written or verbal language. Gardner (1983) proposes that human intelligence has been defined too narrowly. He has distinguished seven kinds of human intelligence: linguistic, musical, logical-mathematical, spatial, bodily kinesthetic, interpersonal, and intrapersonal, and has found that human beings who exhibit intelligence in one domain do not necessarily exhibit intelligence in another. Indeed, it is each person's unique blend of competencies that produces an individual cognitive profile. Thus, as teachers working with learners in an academic context, we need to be aware and respond to this individuality in students learning and demonstrating their knowledge.

Individuals have their own unique and complex systems to acquire, store, and retrieve information. By providing an array of methods and venues for learners to perform and express their evolving understanding, we supply all students with equal opportunities for learning and demonstrating that learning. When students and teachers explore concepts using multiple-learning modalities such as dramatic interpretation, artistic representation, or kinesthetic movement as well as verbal and written language, a learning environment is created in which learners encounter content through one mode and then demonstrate their knowledge through another. In the development of curriculum, we might have students act out a childhood memory and later construct a poem based on that memory. Or, conversely, the childhood memory may first be explored through poetry and then later several students' memories become the basis of a classroom play based on childhood. To use a plethora of student learning experiences and responses addresses the significance of multiple modalities and learning (Eisner, 1985).

Concluding Thoughts

Drama can provide learners with developmentally appropriate instruction through processes such as physical movement, speaking, socializing, and decision making. The acquiring of individual self-esteem is pivotal to a student's potential for academic, social, and psychological well-being. And drama, incorporated into the middle-level curriculum, creates natural opportunities for each student to participate actively. When students are encouraged to join in the learning, they will have greater chances to construct an affirmative sense of self.

Learners acquire understanding through multiple routes where each is able to work with content. In other words, there is no single, correct way to structure a learning episode. Rather, learning will happen when the content is presented in such a way as to allow for the learners to interact with content ideas through different channels such as linguistic, kinesthetic, mathematical, or spatial.

References

Babbitt, Natalie. 1975. *Tuck Everlasting*. New York: Farrar, Straus and Giroux.

Bolton, M. Gavin. 1979. *Towards a Theory of Drama in Education*. London: Longman.

Bruner, Jerome. 1974. "Child's Play." *New Scientist* (April).

Courtney, Richard. 1980. *The Dramatic Curriculum*. New York: Drama Book Specialists.

Csikszentmihalyi, Mihaly. 1990. "Literacy and Intrinsic Motivation." *Daedalus* 119, 115–140.

Csikszentmihalyi, Mihaly, and U. Schiefele. 1992. "Arts Education, Human Development, and the Quality of Experience." In B. Reimer and R. A. Smith (Eds.), *The Arts, Education, and Aesthetic Knowing* (pp. 169–191). Chicago: The University of Chicago Press.

Dacey, John S. 1986. *Adolescents Today*. 3rd ed. Glenview, IL: Scott, Foresman.

Eisner, Elliot W. 1985. *The Educational Imagination: On the Design and Evaluation of School Programs*. 2nd ed. New York: Macmillan.

Erikson, Eric H. 1968. *Identity: Youth and Crisis*. New York: Norton.

Gardner, Howard. 1983. *Frames of Mind: The Theory of Multiple Intelligences*. New York: Basic Books.

———. 1990. *Art Education and Human Development*. Los Angeles: The Getty Center for Education in the Arts.

———. 1993. *Multiple Intelligences*. New York: HarperCollins.

Greene, Maxine. 1992. "Text and Margins." In Goldberg, M. R., and A. Phillips (Eds.), *Arts as Education*. Reprint Series No. 24, Cambridge, MA: Harvard Educational Review.

Jensen, William R., Howard N. Sloane, and K. Richard Young. 1988. *Applied Behavior Analysis in Education*. Englewood Cliffs, NJ: Prentice Hall.

Maslow, Abraham. 1971. *The Farther Reaches of Human Nature*. New York: Viking, 1971.

Merleau-Ponty, Maurice. 1964. *The Primacy of Perception*. Evanston, IL: Northwestern University Press.

Moffett, James. 1983. *Teaching the Universe of Discourse.* Boston: Houghton Mifflin.

Phillips, John L., Jr. 1969. *The Origins of Intellect: Piaget's Theory.* San Francisco: W. H. Freeman.

Piaget, Jean. 1926. *The Language and Thought of the Child,* translated by Marjorie Worden. New York: Harcourt Brace and World. (Original French edition, 1923).

Riley, Richard. 1993. Released Statement. U.S. Secretary of Education, U.S. Department of Education. February 23, 1993. Washington, DC.

Shakespeare, William. 1626. *Hamlet.*

Short, Kathy, and Carolyn Burke. 1991. *Creating Curriculum: Teachers and Students as a Community of Learners.* Portsmouth, NH: Heinemann.

Siks, Geraldine B. 1977. *Drama with Children.* New York: Harper and Row.

———. 1983. *Drama with Children.* New York: Harper and Row.

Smith, J. Lea, and J. Daniel Herring. 1994. "Drama in the Middle Level Classroom: Bringing Content to Life." *Middle School Journal* 26:1, 30–36.

Smith, J. Lea, and Holly A. Johnson. 1993. "Control in the Classroom: Listening to Adolescent Voices." *Language Arts* 70:1, 18–30.

2
Drama's ABCs

Focus Question   **What does a teacher need to know about drama to be able to use it in the classroom?**

A Close-Up of Drama

One small group of middle graders chose to highlight a clip from the 1987 film *The Elephant Man,* based on the play by Bernard Pomerance (1979). This viewing provides a natural opportunity for the class to consider the elements of drama. They point out acting techniques the actor uses to portray a man with a debilitating disease. These include how he lives the role: distorted speech, impeded breathing, and physically challenged movements. The students discuss how types of conflict—within one's self as well as man against society—are developed through the film's action.

The middle-level teacher in this vignette shows her students the elements of dramatization rather than simply talking about them. These students are meeting the *ingredients* of dramatic action firsthand as they watch a contemporary film. This assignment asks students to select a movie for studying the development of characterization. The students view their film selection, identify the different means the actor uses to create his character, and then talk about the effectiveness of the actor's choices. This close-up study of characterization places the students within an everyday context of watching a video to become familiar with dramatic literacy. Topics to study include: plot, conflict, characterization, setting, emotion, and action.

Drama as a Way to Teach

Using drama as a way to teach may be unfamiliar to most of us. We tend to agree that drama would actively involve our students and be worthwhile, but the gap between saying and doing may keep us bound to known instructional strategies. This uncertainty raises several questions. When is drama a valuable instructional strategy? How does a teacher use drama to provide students with a meaningful, concrete opportunity to interact with content? What does a teacher need to know about drama to use it in the classroom?

Dramatic action can be integrated into content instruction in a number of ways. Drama brings content studies to life and sparks an interest in the subject. The key is the teacher's realization that drama is a powerful tool for learning. This make-believe play, based on content, becomes very real and can be guided to meet further learning outcomes. Drama naturally enables the learner to engage in play.

The basic premise teachers need to know as they begin to work with drama for instruction is simple: drama is a means of learning through role playing and problem solving. It is a creative way of using the whole body to transmit and receive information with mind, body, and voice working in collaboration to create a "total picture." Drama, as a learning tool, calls for self-awareness, communication skills, concentration, and group cooperation. To use drama within a classroom context requires a teacher to have a working knowledge of (1) how to create dramatic action, (2) how to facilitate student participation within the dramatic action, and (3) how to discuss and evaluate the dramatic action created.

Creating Dramatic Action

A teacher begins the process of integrating drama into her instruction first by becoming familiar with how to structure dramatic action. A fundamental consideration that serves as an anchoring point in the dramatic lesson is the material—the heart of the process. This material provides the hub for subsequent structuring of the dramatic action. It may be just about anything—a textbook chapter, a book, a poem, a film, a student's writings, a newspaper article, a prop, a historical event, or a photograph. Whatever the material, a story develops around it that has a *who*, a *where*, and a *what*. It is these plot elements that will form the drama action the students will develop. For instance, a photograph from Dorothea Lange's book *American Photographs* (1994), depicting the Depression Era, could serve as source material to develop a dramatization that captures the human element as well as the conflict of this time period. Or in the children's novel *Beyond the Divide* (Lasky, 1983) the protagonist, Meribah, faces the challenge of surviving on her own after her father dies as she travels west on a wagon train.

The Who *of Dramatic Action*

The *who* of the selected material is the character of the dramatic action. It is the character confronting obstacles in life that captures our attention. The action—character dealing with conflict—tells the story. In a drama, the development of a character begins with discovering a character's driving instincts. A character is brought to life through the portrayal of such descriptors as: age, education, cultural and religious background, interests and hobbies, occupation, relationship to other characters, physical appearance and health, state of mind, and personality. Whether they are serious, pathetic, laughable, lovable, or contemptible, they need to be believable and consistent throughout the action. Students participating in the drama will need to have an understanding of the character in order to avoid sterotypes. A believable character creates a reality that extends beyond the drama. Within a drama, there may indeed be multiple characters, but they must respond to each other in natural ways.

The first step in the process of developing a character is to identify life descriptors that will breathe the *who* into the characterization. From this, a character's personality is portrayed through body movements and vocalizations. The character's dominant traits are conveyed through ways of talking and moving. In the Lange photograph example, we would first determine and then identify some basic descriptors in order to create the character in the photograph. This information is called a character profile and serves as the blueprint for how a character will be played. It provides the framework with which to expand a character by considering characteristics, thoughts and attitudes, reasons for behaviors, and responses to situations and people. Creating a profile for the Lange photograph would require choosing and then selecting different human traits that may include: a will to survive, making do, hungry, poor, limited opportunities, large family, and a loving mother. This profile provides the context necessary to create the character's physical and vocal traits. For the Lange photograph, these may include a weary and tired movement, a disheveled appearance, and a determined tone of voice.

To develop a character is a challenge because each character must be clearly defined. This is accomplished through an honest interpretation of the character's physical, social, and pyschological traits, which determines how a character ultimately will be developed throughout the dramatic action. One of the most important dimensions of characterization is the motivation of action, which provides the *what* of dramatic action.

The What of Dramatic Action

In a drama, a character faces a challenge, that is, conflict that provides the action for the playing of the material. Conflict is the element in dramatic action that supplies the motivation for the behavior of the characters. It brings the material to life and sets the course to develop interest in how the characters will move toward resolution. Conflict may be comic or tragic and advances toward a satisfying conclusion.

The potential to develop conflict within the action is necessary if the drama is to be convincing. The conflict may take one of four different forms. One type is the conflict of one character against another. It occurs as characters struggle for the same goal, or are prevented from achieving a goal. In *Beyond the Divide* (Lasky, 1983) the protagonist Meribah attempts to ration food to make it last along the journey west, while Mr. Goodnough tries to horde the food for himself. A dramatic playing of this scene from the book would portray these two characters presenting motives for their actions.

A second type of conflict is a character against society. This presents a character (or may include relationships with other closely associated characters) going up against cultural practices or mainstream society. In the book *Beyond the Divide* Meribah's father, who is Amish, addresses conflict when he chooses to break tradition and leave his community in order to move west. A playing of this story conflict might portray a scene in which Meribah's father addresses his community. The playing may capture the dialogue that might develop between Meribah's father and his fellow Amish community members.

The third type of conflict is a character's struggle against nature. This involves a character's battle with the forces of the universe, which may include the supernatural. For example, in *Beyond the Divide,* the snow provides the conflict when Meribah becomes snowbound. She must overcome many obstacles if she is to survive until the spring thaw. A dramatic interpretation could be a pantomine of Meribah's survival techniques such as building a shelter, hunting for and finding adequate food, and trying to stay warm.

The final type of conflict is when a character may face personal barriers. These barriers—emotional or psychological—are internal struggles the character must reckon with as she attempts to achieve goals. Meribah is torn by conflicting ethical beliefs when forced into a hand-and-fist fight. She is opposed to violence as a means to resolve disputes, yet her life is on the line: what should she do? A portrayal of this internal struggle may involve students in composing a journal entry where Meribah debates her options. These writings may be read aloud as monologue performances. (A monologue is a one-character speech and is a solo performance.)

Conflict is the basis of all drama. It captures the disagreement or collision of issues, feelings, or goals among the characters in a plot's action. The personality of a character is portrayed through physical and vocal reactions to the struggles of the conflict. The *where* of the action contributes to character development and how a conflict may be played. This *where* is the setting of a drama.

The Where *of Dramatic Action*

The *where* of drama is the place or environment in which the characters come up against the conflict. This place is the setting, that is, the physical location where character action is played out. The interaction between characters and setting is critical. The character's response to the setting provides the drama with richer characterization and conflict. Simply, does the character like his environment? And how does a character blend (or not blend) in with this place? The place of action may also provide the drama with playable elements within the setting such as temperature, physical dimensions, lighting conditions, ownership (whose turf is it?), or the character's familiarity with the setting.

Students engaging in a drama session will rely primarily on their imaginations to create the setting. If the drama takes place during a time period other than the present, then the student portraying a character in this *where* must imagine what the dramatic time and place would have been like. As an example, the Lange photograph would require students to have some knowledge of the Depression Era so they can respond truthfully to the environmental conditions of the young mother. To dramatize this photograph, students might create street signs (setting) of products and prices of this era to create a simple set. In turn, the students would need to create appropriate dialogue that reflects the circumstances of this specific time in history. It is important not to pull in contemporary language and references such as referring to a fast food restaurant or using a phrase like, "May the Force be with you."

These elements—the *who*, the *what*, and the *where*—are the questions to be answered in a dramatic playing. They find their definition in the materials (books, photographs, or film) and provide a working design for the action. When a teacher becomes fluent in the basics to creating dramatic action, this knowledge enables her to structure instructional lessons that involve the learners in living the concepts under study. Drama adds action to the content and encourages students to be the actors in the learning process. And it is when they are at the center of action that content comes to life.

Facilitating Student Participation within Dramatic Action

A teacher is able to assist students during a dramatic playing of the materials through the use of two techniques: *side coaching* and *teacher-in-role*. Each of these helps to further encourage and involve the students. When a teacher takes an active role as either a character within the drama or as a guide outside the drama, students tend to be more enthusiastic as they see the teacher "actually doing it so I will too." Yet, a teacher's participation is to inspire students and to show, through active involvement, that the venture is not a time filler but a valid way to learn. This teacher interaction is important, but should not dictate to students how to play characters and conflict. Here is our rule of thumb for how much a teacher should participate: when the students begin to build upon the ideas a teacher has given, then she begins to step back and give verbal encouragement, either in or out of role, when the action lulls. The teacher's sole objective is to act as a mentor who enables students to own the drama activities instead of making the students copy her ideas.

Teacher as Side Coach

Side coaching situates the teacher in a role where she offers words of encouragement or direction as the drama is in progress. This role orchestrates the action through giving instructions and cueing students as needed. The purpose of these sideline comments is to add depth while advancing the action. The teacher as a side coach may fill in awkward silences and give security to students who are hesitating as well as provide focus to those who appear removed and have an attitude of "I don't want to do this."

Side coaching is verbal reinforcement that may take the form of questions, comments, suggestions, and encouragement as well as general observations to point out different ideas. This commentary supplies encouragement to both individual involvement and group participation. For example, dramatization of the novel *Walk Two Moons* (Creech, 1994) could have groups of students depicting different scenes from the story. The teacher circulates among the groups offering verbal comments to point out strong ideas and spur students forward. Examples of side coaching might include:

> I can see the age difference between Salamanca and her grandparents because your energy levels are different for each character and your body and voice are showing these differences.

> Remember—when your group is working on how you will act out the scene, be sure to develop the action around the conflict in that part of the story.

I notice you are aware of the car's confining space at moments in your scene, but at other times you forget and perform actions you just couldn't do in a moving car.

Additionally, the teacher as side coach might be the narrator and read aloud the materials as the students act. The techniques of side coaching help both students and teacher to expand necessary skills in order to create a dramatic context. With practice, the teacher will become more familiar with side coaching along with a perception of the students' developmental needs. The purpose of side coaching is to encourage students through supportive comments. These are most effective when they are not evaluative, but rather formative. By this, we mean the feedback stimulates the students to participate purposefully in the dramatic experience; it is not a form of evaluation. We have found that statements such as "Your characterization is wrong, do it like this. I can't hear you, speak up if you are going to do this. Why are you developing your character like that?" limits students' learning possibilities. Our work with middle-level learners has taught us to use side coaching as an avenue to place the student, rather than the teacher, as the evaluator. When a student begins to self-evaluate the development of a dramatic action, she becomes the "initiator" of the scene.

Teacher-in-Role

The other facilitating technique places the teacher in a role within the dramatic action alongside the students. This is called teacher-in-role. As a way to guide the drama, this technique does not interrupt the action of the drama to provide formative feedback. Dorothy Heathcote, a renowned English drama educator, uses this technique and finds it to be highly effective for leading and directing young people in a drama.

Teacher-in-role is useful when beginning drama work with a class of students. The teacher plays a character role in the drama and through that role is able to respond to students' needs while acting as the character in the action. As teacher-in-role, the teacher is able to give the students a person to respond to. This interaction is live and immediate. Rather than discussing what a character might say or do, the students and teacher play it out. In playing a role, the teacher is not to act in some steretypical or showy manner. Most of us as teacher-in-role will probably suggest more than act out a role. This produces a focus of attention for the students, while the teacher is able to challenge feelings and attitudes of apathy and uncertainty. An example of teacher-in-role we have used with students in a study of the Depression Era is a re-creation of a scene where characters are receiving food. Each student selects a person from Lange's photographic text to develop as a character. To faciliate dramatic action, we (teacher-in-role) assume the character of the person who is managing the food distribution. This provides a natural opportunity for the teacher to keep the action rolling while allowing students to develop their character and play off the teacher-in-role's comments, questions, and overall character. Teacher-in-role is fundamentally a teaching strategy that provides a natural opening for a teacher to co-create learning with her students.

Guiding Students to an Understanding of the Drama Created

Once students have played out a drama, they will need time to think about their actions. The teacher acts as a facilitator to open such a discussion. The focus of the dialogue is the concept underlying the drama lesson. For example, in the playing of *Walk Two Moons* (Creech, 1994), a social studies lesson might build on the trip west. One identified learning outcome could be finding out how to use narrative description to locate sites on a map. The students could trace Salamanca's and her grandparents' travels across the midwest to Idaho. Students, as a group, could chart the trip on a map by using the text descriptions to examine the different geographical areas such as climate, terrain, and other unique physical features. Drama integrates a third dimension to this literature-based map-reading unit. Small groups of students plan a dramatic playing of a scene to depict one of Salamanca's traveling experience's with her grandparents. The students' dramatic portrayals would integrate knowledge from their reading with an understanding of the natural features of a specific location. Once the small groups have played their dramatic interpretation, the teacher initiates an evaluation discussion.

Evaluation is a natural component in all drama activities. This examination provides both the students and the teacher with an opportunity to bring together content, personal experience, and encyclopedic knowledge. By this, we define *content* to encompass knowledge of *what* is being studied as well as the drama techniques. *Personal experience* is the individual student's perceptions and ideas regarding the content. And *encyclopedic knowledge* refers to other peoples' culture, history, and experience. In our *Walk Two Moons* example, you might ask the students to discuss what new information they gleaned about geography from charting the journey on the map. Another focus question would revolve around dramatic techniques such as what physical and vocal qualities they used to create the characters for the improvisations. This discussion would provide a chance for commentary on the content of the *Walk Two Moons* session. A question such as "What experiences have you had that mirror those of the characters in the book?" would provide a jumping-off point for an open-ended discussion using personal perspective as the means for a personal connection to the story. Getting at encyclopedic knowledge can sometimes be difficult, but this type of exploration provides students with a chance to expand their existing knowledge. In this phase of the evaluation focusing on what others think and feel is the primary goal. Questions that probe how history, culture, and environment may influence behavior will bridge content to personal experience to encyclopedic knowledge. The *Walk Two Moons* encyclopedic questioning would ask students to experience Salamanca's feelings of separation and loss. Typical questions might include "In what way does Salamanca learn to accept her mother's death?"; "In what ways do Salamanca's grandparents react differently to her mother's death?", and, "In what ways are the reactions similar and different?"

Figure 2–1 illustrates our approach to designing the evaluation component of a drama lesson.

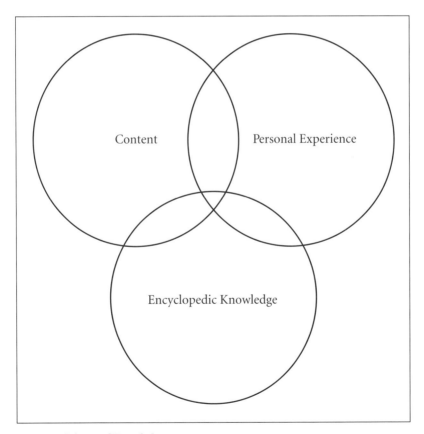

Figure 2–1. *Spheres of Knowledge*

This evaluation phase of the lesson is similar to the type of give and take of a questioning atmosphere among friends. The goal of this group dialogue is to encourage students to generate ideas rather than expecting them to be passive repositories of what the teacher or the book says. The teacher asks students to describe the experience rather than tell them how to respond. Students and teacher are equals, with all of the talk encouraging others to add comments. Such a setting invites active participation in the learning. Given a topic of mutual interest, this climate would spark a dynamic interchange of discussion to foster students' content knowledge while adding both a personal and world perspective.

To design an evaluation questioning strategy requires a teacher to experiment with different approaches to incorporate the three dimensions of knowledge—content, personal experience, and encyclopedic. Our firsthand experience reveals that asking the right questions is a developmental process. You may begin with asking questions from only one of the knowledge spheres. This is okay. To be able to weave together questions from the three sources of knowledge is a trial-and-error operation. And we have found that it takes experience, coupled with a commitment to stay with it, that leads to an encompassing evaluation. It is important for a teacher to continue trying different ideas, discarding those that are ineffective.

In the *Walk Two Moons* drama, the instructional session bringing the three spheres of knowledge together begins with combining two spheres simultaneously such as content and personal experience, or personal experience and encyclopedic knowledge, or encyclopedic knowledge and content. Examples of questions include: "On Salamanca's trip west, she saw different sights and people. Now, think of a trip you have taken. This can be any type of trip, even a car ride to a neighboring city. You noticed different people and sights. Describe some of these. In what way did the people seem to fit in with their environment?" (content knowledge and personal experience); "Now think of a person you know, and place that person as a character in *Walk Two Moons*. How would this "transferred" person respond to the experiences within the story?" (personal experience and encyclopedic knowledge); and "In the story the characters were on a car trip to Idaho. They relied on road maps to chart their route. How is a map made? What types of information would a mapmaker need in order to create a map?"(content knowledge and encyclopedic knowledge).

Combining the different ways of knowing, that is, the three knowledge spheres, provides learners with an integrated curriculum in which the different ways of knowing become interrelated. By this we mean that encyclopedic knowledge is as relevant to personal experience as it is to content. An encompassing curriculum blends these three knowledge spheres together and allows for the world of school to be connected to the world outside. In our *Walk Two*

Moons instructional episode, a content theme could be separation and loss. This focus becomes the basis from which to develop questions that unite the three spheres of knowledge. Questions might include: "You experience the loss of a classmate who has been killed in an auto accident. In what ways would your personal reactions likely be similar to other students and teachers? How might they be different? And how might your school community accommodate this loss?" The questioning strategy creates a context in which students bridge from the content of the text to their personal experience with death, to their encyclopedic knowledge regarding how others may handle the death of a classmate.

Concluding Thoughts

In this chapter, we present the *who, what,* and *where* of incorporating drama into the middle-level curriculum. A fundamental point of reference is a teacher's willingness to play with the ABCs of dramatic action as a way for her to teach and for her students to learn. These drama abcs include (1) creating dramatic action; (2) facilitating students' participation within dramatic action; and (3) guiding students to an understanding of the dramatic action.

A natural outcome is that of a teacher, along with her students, learning the basics of theater. This understanding involves a knowledge of how to develop characterization, conflict, and setting. Knowledge of these drama concepts is not difficult to understand nor to use in an instructional episode.

Another outcome of a teacher incorporating dramatic content instruction is a learning situation in which students have multiple opportunities to consider the human condition as it relates to the larger world around them. It is this dramatic approach to curriculum—making a classroom a place where the events occurring beyond the walls of the school are a natural dimension of content—that creates greater student involvement and subsequently, the acquisition of knowledge—learning.

Dramatic content instruction creates a setting where the real actors, the students, are given useful techniques to comprehend their reality, and in turn allows them to play, through drama, how they wish to present themselves to this reality.

References

Creech, Sharon. 1994. *Walk Two Moons*. New York: HarperCollins Publishers.

Lange, Dorothea. 1994. *American Photographs*.

Lasky, Kathryn. 1983. *Beyond the Divide*. New York: Macmillan.

Pomerance, Bernard. 1979. *The Elephant Man: A Play*. New York, Grove Press.

3
Making Learning
a Dramatic Experience

"*Drama offers a way of putting meaning into action and action into meaning, providing a rehearsal for living that aids in sensitizing participants to the world around them.*"

RUTH BEALL HEINIG, 1994
CREATIVE DRAMATIST

Focus Question **What are the methodologies for structuring classroom drama?**

A Close-Up of Drama

Eighth-grade students on B team have read *Nothing But the Truth* (Avi, 1991), an adolescent novel. Ms. Johnson has outlined a linear drama plan for her second period language arts class. Her instructional strategy has the students first exploring the physical and vocal dimensions of the story characters. After this warm-up, students working in small groups will act out selected dialogue passages from the text.

Across the hall, Mr. Casey, *in role* as superintendent of schools, welcomes his second period social studies students. He initiates his holistic drama session by handing his students a court order requiring all students to say the Pledge of Allegiance each morning and to stand in reverence during the playing of the national anthem. Students drop into role and begin to question the superintendent regarding the ruling.

Both teachers are using drama as a means to explore the layers of meaning in *Nothing But the Truth* (Avi, 1991). Ms. Johnson's linear drama session was primarily planned and outlined prior to involving her students, whereas Mr. Casey's holistic drama session built on an improvisational framework that asked his students to drop into character and assume a role without dramatic

24

preparation. Both linear and holistic drama allow opportunities for students to engage in dramatic activities that create an instructional setting where students approach content through action. This results in an opportunity to make unique and individual contributions to their learning through drama. One dramatic structure—*linear*—provides the teacher with a sequential step-by-step approach, while the other—*holistic*—provides the teacher with a process framework.

Structuring Classroom Drama Activities

The middle-level teacher faces the challenge of creating an instructional environment that bridges what students know and what they want to know (Cooter & Chilcoat, 1990). Beane (1992) states that genuine learning involves an interaction between the learner, the environment, and the content. This interaction integrates what we experience into our system of meanings. Drama can initiate this interaction. It creates a learning setting that enables students to live through content information in a way that can only deepen their understanding of and their appreciation for content information and concepts. Furthermore, drama is action in the present—"action" that prevents academic content from appearing dry, lifeless, abstract and beyond understanding. Piaget (1979) points out that physical activity can become the groundwork for abstract mental concepts. Drama empowers students to learn new knowledge and also, as Gavin Bolton (1984) has noted, enables them to understand more deeply what they already know.

Although as teachers we may recognize the power of combining drama, learning, and students, extended dramatization is still a relatively rare event in most middle-level classrooms. But this doesn't have to be the case. When a teacher decides to "play" with drama as an instructional strategy, there are basically two approaches—linear and holistic—that work most effectively.

Linear Drama Approach

One way to initate drama in middle-level studies is through a linear approach (Ward, 1957). A middle-level teacher initiating drama into his classroom for the first time may prefer the linear structure. With this structure, drama activities are primarily planned and outlined by the teacher before involving the students in the dramatic playing. This tends to give the teacher greater control while allowing creative input from the students. The linear drama session resembles a recipe, with a series of steps that produce a selected learning outcome. These stages include planning, playing, evaluating, and optionally, replaying.

Planning Stage

The first stage begins with selecting a theme or concept for the students to explore through drama. This theme may reflect content concepts under study as well as issues or conflicts presented in content readings, or it may build on students' interests. Poems, short stories, textual passages, or original improvisations drawn from content are suitable materials. The materials build on the theme and provide opportunities to extend learning.

The teacher outlines a strategy for engaging the students with the materials used in the dramatic playing. A good beginning point for developing a linear session is to focus on the physical characterization of the theme or concept (Siks, 1983). In one of our linear drama session examples, the unifying theme is insects, which we explore through creative movement and poetry (see Figure 3–1). Motivating and focusing the students for dramatic

---

I. Topic: Exploring physical and vocal interpretation

II. Issues of Exploration: Insect characterization, group cooperation, communication through dramatization

III. Focusing Question: What are the many ways we use our bodies and voices to communicate ideas and feelings?

IV. Planning

Warmup

Students listen to appropriate music while the teacher uses guided imagery to assist the students in visualizing an insect character of their choosing. This includes verbally walking the students through the transformation from a person to an insect.

Teacher Dialogue

"In your own space with your eyes closed, think about how your body can become the body of your insect. What can you do with your arms? Show me. Now, show me what your legs would look like. Don't forget that your face is a part of your physical character. Now, as the music continues to play, move around the room and explore it as the insect would." The students will move through the space as their chosen insect.

Figure 3–1. *Example of a Linear Drama Session*

V. Playing

Sharing of the material

The teacher reads "House Crickets" (Fleischman, 1988).

Trying-On

The teacher uses guided imagery to assist the students in picturing a cricket in their minds. In their own space, students pose as a cricket. When the teacher gives a signal (hand clap), the cricket statues come to life and move about the playing area. After this, the teacher signals the students to add sound effects to their cricket characterizations.

Dramatization

Students are placed in groups of about five. Each small group of students is given a section of the poem "House Crickets" (Fleischman, 1988) to develop for a large-group presentation. The working groups are given ample time to prepare. Each group then presents their portion of the poem in sequential order, which constitutes the large-group playing. The small group's enactment may be done in several ways: one person reading, two voices reading, choral reading, or dual voices as group members perform their stanza dramatization.

VI. Evaluation

After the dramatization, the teacher and students discuss the experience. This discussion focuses on interpretations and characterizations that were effective as well as drama skills that were used in developing the dramatizations.

VII. Replaying and Follow-up

The same groupings of students may be given a copy of the poem "Fireflies" (Fleischman, 1988) for developing a second dramatization. After the groups work through how they will handle verse reading, characterization, and physical interpretations, they share their dramatization with the class. The group discusses the interpretations, characterizations, and other drama elements including sound, movement, sense awareness, concentration, and group cooperation, which may vary considerably.

Figure 3–1. *Example of a Linear Drama Session*

activities is essential. The warm-up moves students through physical activities that loosen the body and uses visual imagery activities to encourage mental concentration. Students' performance skills include voice, sense awareness, movement, memory, and characterization. In this example, the warm-up uses guided imagery to help students physically create an insect.

The teacher's role during a linear drama session is usually as narrator, or side coach: the teacher orchestrates the action by giving instructions and cueing students as needed. He may also narrate the text that is part of the dramatic activity and help students stay focused on their respective roles.

Playing Stage

The teacher begins this stage by sharing the material to be dramatized with his students. Methods for sharing include reading, telling, or choral reading. For original improvisations, descriptive instructions focus on character, setting, and dramatic action. After sharing the material, the teacher leads students through a trying-on of the characters. This provides an opportunity for the students to become acquainted with the characters to be dramatized. The trying-on is structured so that students briefly encounter life as the character, enabling them to find the elements of voice and body that work in portraying the character. In the insect lesson example, students explore their space as a cricket.

After the trying-on, the selected dramatic material is brought to life with the students developing the theme through their dramatic actions. This can be done in a number of ways. Small groups might act out a particular section of the material or small groups might dramatize the entire piece. Or the group as a whole could enact parts or the entire piece. The playing also may be structured as duet dramatization. In our cricket example, students are divided into small groups where they develop a dramatic enactment of a stanza of the verse, which the small groups then perform sequentially as part of the whole-group dramatization.

Evaluation Stage

Involving students in assessment encourages reflective analysis of their learning experience. The content of the dramatic session guides the evaluation that may involve discussing topics related to concepts of language arts, science, math, foreign language, or social studies. During this reflective evaluation, students discuss their personal reaction, the content and theme, and how they can extend the experience or skills to other situations, including actual circumstances. At this point students also discuss their varying uses of dramatic skills such as voice, movement, character, and conflict.

Replay Stage

A linear session may employ a replay stage following the evaluation stage. This permits further development of the initial dramatization by incorporating observations from the evaluation into further playings. This stage might involve a second enactment of the first dramatization, a new drama using other materials, or a continued playing of the original drama. (See Figures 3–1 and 3–2 for linear drama sessions.)

Another linear drama session is utilized as a way to extend the issues raised in the story book *Something Upstairs* (Avi, 1988), as described in Figure 3–2.

I. Topic: Examining the issues related to slavery in American history

II. Issues of Exploration: Personal story as history; conditions of friendship; loyalty to self and others; racial prejudice

III. Focusing Questions: What are our responsibilties for the human condition? What was life like for an African slave in the 1800s?

IV. Planning

- Divide the class into two groups on opposite sides of the classroom.
- Involve one group as Kenny who wants to help Caleb, and the other group as Kenny who doesn't wish to help. Allow this dramatic debate between the two sides of Kenny's character to examine his possible thoughts, feelings, and behaviors. This debate lasts from 5 to 7 minutes.
- Involve the groups as the character Caleb in a similar dramatic debate: one group as Calebs who want to leave history as it is, and the other as Calebs who want to rewrite history.
- Pair the students. One student is assigned the character Caleb and the other, Kenny. In role as characters, the students participate in a written dialogue activity. In written dialogue, the characters communicate to each other through writing. One character writes a note and hands it to the other character who reads it and then writes a response, which is returned to the other. For example, the character Caleb writes "Caleb: 'Please help me!'" The character Kenny writes "Kenny: 'Who are you? Where'd you

---

Figure 3–2. *Example of a Linear Drama Session (continued on page 30)*

come from?'" This written dialogue continues for 10 to 12 minutes and is the beginnings of a scene the pair will act out.

V. Playing

Rehearsal

Using the written dialogue as a departure, the pair improvises a scene between Caleb and Kenny that addresses the thoughts, feelings, and behaviors of each character. Encourage the pair to review the book in order to present a scene that includes why Caleb and Kenny become friends in a time in history when blacks and whites most likely did not have personal friendships. This rehearsal period may vary, but a minimum of one class period will be needed.

Presentation

Provide a time for each pair to present their Kenny and Caleb scene.

VI. Evaluation and Follow-Up

- Lead a discussion that centers on (1) our responsibilty to create a world where equality rings true, and (2) the differences and similarities between a slave's life in the 1800s and a minority person's life in the 1990s.
- Select, with the students, other historical happenings to rewrite alternative outcomes to the particular event. The rewriting could involve students in organizing a scripted scene for dramatization.

Figure 3–2. *Example of a Linear Drama Session*

Holistic Drama

In contrast to the linear approach, the basic holistic method has students dropping into a role at the gut level (Wagner, 1976) without instruction in dramatic skills. Students are encouraged to live the invented life (of the drama) in an improvisational framework, creating an element of surprise that can lead to a new awareness or understanding. In a holistic session, students assume the attitudes of a character, display external actions that symbolize internal meaning, and develop an understanding of the themes, values, and issues of the material enacted (Wright and Herring, 1987). Teacher-in-role is a key element in holistic drama. The teacher takes on a role as a character within the improvised drama, which helps focus the students' attention while challenging feelings and attitudes of apathy and uncertainty. This unites them in problem solving and propels them into action (O'Neill, 1991).

The tableau or frozen picture is another effective strategy in holistic drama. By stopping the action, students gain an opportunity to reflect on what has happened in the dramatization and plan for what may occur next. During the tableau, the teacher supplies the students with comments or questions to develop their character, examine their characters' emotional states, and propel the students into the next episode or scene.

Planning a holistic drama session begins with the identification of a theme that is selected jointly by both the teacher and the students. The holistic episode might be to examine some aspect of the curriculum being studied. An example is to explore the depths of the oceans as part of a science unit. Once the theme is identified, the teacher studies the topic and prepares dramatic structures that provide focused learning episodes for playing, including the development of the role the teacher will play during the improvised drama.

In one of our holistic drama examples, the theme for exploration is the voyage of Christopher Columbus in 1492 (see Figure 3–3). We begin by studying the man and his time using an adolescent literature thematic text set that includes *Christopher Columbus* (Osborne, 1987) and *The Story of Christopher Columbus* (Osborne, 1987). Other resource materials include *Rethinking Columbus* (Bigelow, Miner, and Peterson, 1992) and *Foreigners: A Play of Christoforo Columbus* (Schlitz, 1991). The teacher reviews the literature and chooses passages that will generate the most playable dramatic action. These become dramatic structures that will be developed by the students and teacher. Opportunities to develop an original character and experience

---

I. Objective: To create a historical event through dramatization; to develop realistic three-dimensional characters and walk in their shoes.

II. Structures

Structure I

Tableau

Students sit with their eyes closed, and the teacher explains that they are crew members on the voyage of Columbus in 1492. The

---

Figure 3–3. *Example of a holistic drama session (continued on page 32)*

teacher guides them in visualizing the crew member they have chosen to portray the character. The guided imagery could include known historical facts, suggestions for character development, and establishment of the setting that initiates the dramatization.

Playing

Students board the ship (designated playing area) with their gear. Columbus, the teacher in role, welcomes them aboard, gives directions for storing their gear, and encourages them to become acquainted with the different areas of the ship. Then Columbus answers their questions about the voyage ahead. The action of the characters is spontaneous and develops as the structure is played.

Structure II

Tableau

After the question-and-answer scene is played out completely, the teacher freezes the action and steps out of role. In this tableau, the teacher reports on the first days of a successful voyage—beautiful weather, bountiful supplies, and smooth sailing ahead.

Playing

Crew members are celebrating at a banquet in honor of Columbus. Crew members salute Columbus, acknowledging him as a great admiral. These unrehearsed acknowledgements may be short speeches, cheers, saluatory comments, or whatever evolves as the scene is played.

Structure III

Tableau

The teacher propels the students into creating the mood of an unhappy crew ready for mutiny. Information used to create this mood includes the description of a longer journey than anticipated, announcement of rationed supplies, and recalling the bad weather that damaged one of the ships. Students have time to reflect on this information before action resumes.

Figure 3–3. *Example of a holistic drama session*

Playing

Crew members begin the scence boisterously, demanding an audience with Columbus. They shout and chant their demands until Columbus appears and a confrontration occurs between the crew members and Columbus. This scene continues until Columbus refuses to answer and leaves the main deck.

Structure IV

Tableau

The teacher suggests that the crew has come to a state of despair and doom, culminating in fear that death at sea is imminent.

Playing

Disheartened crew members bemoan their doom. They speak of their homeland, families, and curse their unfulfilled dream of wealth and fame. The dramatization is open to allow each student to respond as their character might in these circumstances. As the structure evolves, land is sighted by Columbus, who calls to his crew. An impromptu celebration unfolds.

Evaluation: Following the playing of the four structures, the group reflects on and discusses the experience from both a personal and third-person perspective. Using these different perspectives encourages students to look at historical context as well as historical figures portrayed as three-dimensional characters.

Figure 3–3. *Example of a holistic drama session*

varying emotional states associated with the 1492 voyage are desirable features in selecting passages. Examples of playable passages include boarding the ship and meeting Christopher Columbus, celebrating after several days of smooth sailing, confronting Columbus after many grueling weeks at sea, and sighting land. Before playing structure 1 (Figure 3–3), the tableau technique is used to get the students into role. Stopping the action would be used to move students from one structure to the next and allows the teacher to step out of the dramatic role and coach the students. For example, during the tableau following structures 2 and 3 the teacher enhances the dramatic action by describing the bad weather experienced, the damaged ship, and rationed supplies. In our example, the teacher orchestrates playing of the structures in the role of Christopher Columbus.

I. Objective: To examine the possible advantages or disadvantages of living forever; to develop a character who expresses a full range of emotions; to explore biophysical issues.

II. Structures

Structure I

Tableau

In order to create a setting in which students will critically think through the issues involved in living forever, the teacher, through narration, describes a revolutionary scientific experiment. This experiment has discovered a drug that significantly slows the aging process and allows people to live forever. In this guided imagery, the teacher describes the students as willing participants in this scientific experiment. They are at the lab to sign consent letters and be administered the experimental drug. As participants in this scientific study, students are encouraged to think of questions to ask the scientist and legal personnel in charge of the drug study.

Playing

Students are waiting in the lab for the scientist and legal personnel to arrive. The scientist—teacher-in-role—welcomes the study participants, introduces the legal personnel (a person who has been previously designated), and invites their questions. During the question-and-answer session, the participants are asked to sign the circulating consent letter. The action of the characters is spontaneous and unfolds as the structure is played with the drug being administered at the close of the structure. The drug is a candy such as a Smartie, M&M, or Life Saver.

Structure II

Tableau

The action is frozen. In this tableau, the teacher reports that ten years have passed. The participants have assembled at the lab for a report on their progress. During this meeting between the legal personnel, the scientist, and the study group the discussion centers on events that have taken place during the previous ten years.

Figure 3–4. *An example of a holistic drama session*

Playing

The study group is waiting in the lab. Scientist and legal personnel arrive. The group begins to discuss exploring such questions as "Think about what has changed or remained the same in your life. Where are you living? How have relationships with family and friends changed? Has the drug enhanced your physical or mental ability? What plans do you have for the future?" This scene is thoroughly played and an announcement is made that the next scheduled meeting will be in ten years. The teacher steps out of role and action is frozen.

Structure III

Tableau

The teacher moves the students into this structure, where they have been requested to come immediately to the lab after only two years have lapsed. After receiving an unexpected phone call, study participants are anxious as they gather at the lab to await the arrival of the scientist and legal personnel. The group has been kept waiting for over an hour. Students are given time to reflect on this before action resumes. This reflection allows for an uncertain tone to develop.

Playing

Pensive study participants are discussing why they have been called together and what this meeting could possibly be about. The scientist and the legal personnel enter and announce that the effects of the drug seem to be altered. Rather than halting the aging process, the drug is working in reverse—it is speeding it up! Based on emerging results of studies with animals, the test animals have started to age rapidly. The last test animal died approximately one hour ago, which suggests that life expectancy is 15 to 20 years after taking the drug. On hearing this announcement, the participants begin to respond spontaneously. The scene continues until the scientist and the legal personnel inform the participants to put their affairs in order and that they will meet again before they die, which appears to be two years away.

Figure 3–4. *An example of a holistic drama session (continued on page 36)*

Structure IV

Tableau

The teacher informs the participants that they have returned one last time to the lab. At this time, participants have approximately one month to live.

Playing

While the participants wait for the scientist and the legal personnel to arrive, they write statements that capture their personal feelings throughout the scientific experiment. Once the playing begins, the participants share their statements with the scientist and legal personnel. The scene ends when the participants submit their personal narratives.

Evaluation:

As closure to this holistic session, students and teacher examine the dramatic experience through a discussion of issues surrounding the concept of immortality. This discussion would look at both the benefits as well as the drawbacks. Other topics for discussion may include medical testing on animals, and the range of emotions each of us exhibits throughout our lives. The use of multiple perspectives surrounding an issue can also be a central focus for the evaluation of this holistic drama.

Figure 3–4. *An example of a holistic drama session*

Another approach to develop a holistic drama session is to focus on a theme or topic. In our example, a class of eighth-grade students examines the topic of immortality.

Concluding Thoughts

Both linear and holistic drama can potentially enrich and sustain students' understanding not only through the development of their own dramatic interpretations, but also in contemplating the work of their peers. Providing opportunities for learners to engage in dramatic activities produces an environment where students' attitudes toward learning improve. This improvement is a result of the opportunity to make unique and individual contributions to their learning through drama. The holistic drama structure provides the teacher with a flexible framework, while the linear drama structure provides the teacher with a sequential step-by-step approach. Both provide the teacher with a tool for an active approach to content.

References

Avi. 1991. *Nothing but the Truth.* New York: Orchard Books.

———. 1988. *Something Upstairs.* New York: Orchard Books.

Beall Heinig, Ruth. 1994. "Reading, Literature, and the Dramatic Language Arts" in *Reading Process and Practice* by C. Weaver. 2nd ed., 437– 477. Portsmouth: NH.

Beane, James A. 1992. "Turning the Floor Over: Reflections on a Middle School Curriculum." *Middle School Journal,* 34 – 40.

Bolton, Gavin. 1979. *Towards a Theory of Drama in Education.* London: Longman.

Bolton, Gavin. 1984. *Drama as Education.* New York: Longman.

Cooter, R. B., and G. W. Chilcoat. 1990. "Content-Focused Melodrama: Dramatic Renderings of Historical Text." *Journal of Reading* 34, 274 – 277.

Fleischman, Paul. 1988. *Joyful Noise.* New York: Harper and Row.

Haskins, Jim. 1990. *Christopher Columbus: Admiral of the Ocean Sea.* New York: Scholastic.

Herring, J. Daniel, and J. Lea Smith. 1991. "Bringing Content To Life." Presentation at the 1991 National Middle School National Conference, Louisville, KY.

Johnson, L., and Cecily O'Neill. (Eds.) 1984. *Dorothy Heathcote: Collected Writings on Drama and Education.* London: Hutchinson.

Osborne, M. P. 1987. *The Story of Christopher Columbus.* New York: Dell.

O'Neill, Cecily. 1991. "Dramatic Worlds: Structuring for Significant Experience." *Drama Theatre Teacher,* 3 – 5.

Schlitz, Laura A. 1991. *A Play of Christoforo Colombo.* Unpublished play manuscript.

Siks, Geraldine B. 1983. *Drama with Children.* New York: Harper and Row.

Wadsworth, B. J. 1979. *Piaget's Theory of Cognitive Development.* New York: Longman.

Wagner, Betty J. 1976. *Dorothy Heathcote: Drama as a Learning Medium.* Washington, DC: National Education Association.

Wright, Lin, and J. Daniel Herring. 1987. "The Arts Approach to Holistic Drama at Arizona State University." *Drama Contact* 11, 3 – 6.

4
Dramatizing a Story

"Indeed, literature is the perfect fabric for creative dramatics, for it is closest to drama and to life itself."

WINIFRED WARD, 1952[1]

Focus Question   What are the benefits of dramatizing literature?

A Close-Up of Drama

Student groups are acting out scenes from the storybook *Pink and Say* (Polacco, 1994). Mr. Easton has coached his students to develop improvisations of storybook scenes to provide them with an opportunity to live the literary action as a play. Each of the different groups has been assigned a specific scene from the storybook to prepare. During the playing, the story is portrayed in sequential order. Scenes depicted may include Pink and Say's meeting; Moe Moe Bay caring for Say; the death of Moe Moe Bay, and the capture of Pink and Say by the Confederate Army.

Story Dramatization

Dramatizing a storybook offers a lens to view the literary action. Story dramatization of literature has students using the literary plot line as the guiding force to create an informal play. This task provides students with an opening to view, through action, the events of the storybook. Students walk in the shoes of their character, speak their words, and may feel their emotions as they bring to life the drama from the pages of the book.

We will provide, in this chapter, the *how-to* of story dramatization. Our step-by-step procedure will show the stages in portraying a book through informal and improvised dramatic action. The action begins when a teacher recognizes the learning possibilities arising from combining literature and drama as a way to learn as well as a way to teach. The literary plot line serves as the basis of the improvised script. This fundamental consideration—liter-

38

ature as the script—is central to dramatizing a story. The words of the story-book serve as the prompt for the dialogue and action. It is important that the storybook is used as the dramatic action rather than as a resource for creating other drama responses or curriculum studies. The book is the script in story dramatization.

The purpose of informal improvisation differs from those of a formal theatrical production. Informal dramatic action is an instantaneous response, whereas a formal production is a series of rehearsals of a published script. The outcome of informal improvisation is the participants' involvement with creating the story as a play as opposed to performing a script for an audience. The students' natural play response is the determining variable in story improvisation. Story dramatization brings a story to life in the present moment.

Spontaneous dramatic performance has the potential to fortify students' learning as they live the learning. This active learning revolves around creative thinking, problem solving, and individual response—process skills essential to the many life situations a student faces. Additionally, informal improvisation furnishes concrete encounters in how to interact socially as well as working cooperatively.

Drama—story enactment—provides a context where students have opportunities to pause, reflect, and portray an other's viewpoint. This opportunity to consider the multiple avenues of social interaction offers students chances to learn distinct social skills. These would include opportunities to think and respond in the heat of the moment—to think on your feet; to express ideas clearly and succinctly, with all voices being heard and considered; to command impassioned emotion for effective communication; and to learn how to enjoy oneself and have fun with learning different ways to socialize. Students' portrayal of different historical figures, literary plots, or contemporary themes puts a face on a study of the human condition.

Dramatic enactment of story brings content to life. And when students are given an opportunity to walk in the shoes of learning, their learning becomes tangible—information they may draw upon to live their lives. Should this not be the underlying locus of our teaching?

The Backdrop for Story Dramatization

The decisive ingredient in story dramatization is opportunity, the chance for students to explore the creative possibilities of the what if? The classroom needs to be a setting where divergent thinking and creative possibilities are encouraged. Classroom story dramatization will be effective only in this accepting environment. Story dramatization builds on a congenial classroom atmosphere where both teachers and students are free to explore the many possibilities to interpret a story. A teacher takes the lead by encouraging and accepting each student's response, and in turn students feel the essential—a security to explore the probable. This does not mean that students who become attention seekers by offering off-the-subject responses are shut down by a "No," but rather redirects them to focus on the topic at hand. Our classroom experiences reveal students who are eager to participate when they are allowed to offer input as to how a story may be dramatized.

The teacher's role is one of helping students feel a sense of security, within the dramatic action, where they know their contributions will be accepted. Students, at all ages, are capable of creating a story play, but this is accomplished only when an allowing attitude induces them to share their ideas openly. A classroom tone that allows students' exploration of possibilities creates a learning setting where story dramatization is the agency to consider the imaginable.

Our classroom experiences reinforce the teacher's pivotal influence in story dramatization. If a teacher is accepting yet nudging, students will respond to dramatizing a story as an opportunity to make believe and respond naturally. This attitude of pretending—playing with the possible—is intrinsic to all curricular instruction. Igniting the imagination happens more readily when students have numerous opportunities to consider multiple ways of interpretating. Multiple ways of being stimulates eager participants in dramatic story playings where consideration of the improbable yet possible is an option. For example, students could walk to the cafeteria as if they were attending a formal dinner reception; during class, when the teacher says to transform, they continue their activities as animal characters; or they may discuss a curriculum topic as persons from a different era. Periodic dramatic moments like these create an environment where students' imaginations are aroused to view the world from a differing perspective. These stepping stones deviate from everyday routines and will allow students to create far more in-depth story dramatizations. And it is this playing with the imagination—considering the improbable that will nurture our students' ability to think beyond the known—which is a fundamental learning outcome.

Presenting the Story

A story dramatization begins with the telling or reading of a story. We find telling the story to younger children to be a more inviting prompt for their dramatizations. It is essential to adapt the story by using your own choice of words when telling a tale. We also may do some editing when we read the story to provide a particular spotlight on the action of the plot. Whether telling or reading a story, the presentation must be sensible, understandable, and focused. Streamlining the story supports the students' grasp of the storyline and ultimately their ability to adapt the story to dramatic action.

A Storyteller's Approach

There are two basic rules to storytelling:

Rule Number One. A storyteller needs to create mental pictures of the story's visual images. By this we mean that you see the story in your head as you tell it. This allows your audience to see the story with their ears. In other words, your telling the story brings it to life.

Rule Number Two. A storyteller creates each character with distinctive traits. These may include a simple change of voice and a physical gesture or movement to give identity to the different characters. This symbolic characterization allows your listeners to identify and follow the characters throughout the story by adding life to the literary text.

A Reader's Approach

Reading a story aloud incorporates two basic approaches:

Rule Number One. Reading a story aloud before sharing it with students is essential. This preparation allows a reader to notice unfamilar words or concepts, unusual language, and repeating phrases. It also frees a reader from total dependence on the text during the oral reading to create more face-to-face interaction with the students.

Rule Number Two. Readers who use their voice to create mood and feelings, to depict different characters, and to speak with clarity and volume make a storybook more engaging than those who read in a monotone, never-changing voice (Sims, 1977).

Telling or reading a story demands genuine enthusiasm—energy in sharing a story is fundamental. This charisma in sharing a story creates a setting where students hang on each word as the tale's climax unfolds. Other tools to use in story sharing are (1) a varied pace and (2) direct address to listeners as the tale is told.

We find it more effective to tell or read the story as it might be dramatized. This direct approach leads to students first listening to the story and then developing the dramatization. The bottomline of story sharing is to establish a pleasurable, inviting environment where listeners are propelled into living the story. The storyteller, or reader, accomplishes this by building a sense of anticipation, marvel, and tension in her listeners.

The Discussion

Our experiences suggest that before sharing a story, the teacher asks students to listen for a particular person, place, thing, or event in the tale. This listening point then becomes a natural entry into discussing the story-sharing episode. For example, you may ask, "What do you think a flower fairy might look like? See if you can picture the flower fairy in your mind's eye." "Why do you think the troll may attempt to stop the goats from crossing the bridge?" "How might Cinderella act when the prince asks her to try on the glass slipper?"

In this way, the story is first shared. Then we follow up with different discussions that provide a place where students are invited to explore the layers of the story. One type of discussion deals with character analysis, which provides a context in which students have an opportunity to try on a character and tease apart differing dimensions of portrayal. Characteristics such as voice, unique movement, emotion, and personality are played with as students discover what a character may or may not be like. It is through discussion that our students have opportunities to cast themselves as a character such as Fudge, Ramona Quimby, the Cat in the Hat, or Huck Finn. Each trying on creates a specific situation where action captures the essence of the character. Examples may include Fudge swallowing Peter's pet turtle with an after burp, Ramona wiggling into a dress for Aunt Bea's wedding, the Cat in the Hat juggling objects in the house, and Huck fishing on the riverbank. This character improvisation allows students to get a feel for a particular story character and is primary to story dramatization. When students are encouraged to try on characters through discussion and physical interpretation, they develop a more in-depth understanding of the character. This leads to greater student participation because the students' imaginations have been warmed up by this initial story improvisation.

Another strategy we use with students is a discussion of the story. This might highlight

1. the plot
2. the primary theme and secondary themes
3. the link between the story and their personal lives
4. character motivation
5. the conflict of the plot

A few examples from our classroom experience include discussing the central issue examined in *James and the Giant Peach* (Dahl, 1988); and in *Jack and the Beanstalk,* students examine a character's actions and discuss whether they are justified. We find students often provide their own questions about why characters make certain choices within the context of the story. For example, one student asked the question in response to *Tom Sawyer*, "what is the importance of telling or not telling secrets?" Student-generated questions frequently become the questions on which we focus the story discussion. Discussing the story is most effective when there is a healthy dose of student directing—students raising questions about the actions in the story and how they, the students, might play a scene. Questioning sets the stage for students to consider differing elements of the story, which ultimately leads to a dramatization with greater depth and more genuineness. It also nurtures more interest and participation by all students. This setting—where all students are acting—is the critical issue.

Planning the Dramatization

A story dramatization has its beginnings in the questions students pose during a story discussion. In the act of discussing the story—plot, characters, action—the story reenactment begins to grow. Initiating a story reenactment revolves around the students' ideas as to how to act out the storyline. And it is from these student suggestions that the story dramatization takes shape.

To guide the developing dramatization, we raise such questions as: "Where in the story will we begin our dramatization?", "What area of the classroom will we use as our playing space?", "What actions will occur to begin the playing of the story?", "What scenes do we play to capture the essence of the story?", "Will the dramatic action tell the story?", "If we are telling a story through actions, how might we show the conflict in the chosen scenes?", and "How will we end the dramatization?" This open-ended setting, where teacher and students discuss possible options for the story dramatization, is fundamental. If story dramatization is to be an opportunity for students to interact with the story, it is then paramount to use the *how, when, where*, and *why* as the guiding parameters to develop the creative process.

Playing Area

The area in which the dramatization takes place is the playing space. This area may be any section of the classroom that fits with how the story will be played. J. Daniel often asks students to "push back the desks" in order to set up a large open area for the dramatization. We also find that with particular story enactments, the dramatization may use the entire classroom space, yet other dramatizations may use a small space within the classroom. A playing area will vary according to the dramatic requirement of the story. In discussing how to present the story, students, along with their teacher, consider the various possibilities of how to use different areas in their classroom to serve as a setting in the story. Representative scenes from *Treasure Island* (Stevenson, 1883) could be played in different areas of the classroom. For example, several desks, arranged in the shape of a boat, could be the playing space for boat scenes. These boat scenes would take place inside the perimeter of the desks, while the island scenes would be played outside this area using the remainder of the classroom space.

The key to establishing a playing space in the classroom for story dramatization is to use the classroom as a place to share rather than as a stage to perform. Story dramatization is a *process activity* in which students interact with the story through improvisation. This student engagement with story, through dramatization, provides the means to live the story as a way to learn.

Who Plays Whom

After the teacher and the students discuss the story, they decide how they will play it. During this planning, students consider different possibilities for where they might play the story within the classroom. At this point, students and teacher begin to sort out who will play which character. Our experience emphasizes the importance of student choice. When students volunteer to play a part, this act of self-choice establishes a setting where they want to be a part of the dramatic action. It is this personal investment in playing a particular character that allows dramatization to become a learning experience centered around literature, improvisation, *and* the students. If a student doesn't volunteer it doesn't mean he or she will not play a part in the story dramatization. Often we find students who want to play a character yet don't volunteer. The teacher should encourage these students to play a role, but not force them. Lea has found it helpful to develop the story dramatization in such a way that all students have a role, whether as an individual character or as a group character. In *Where the Wild Things Are* (Sendak, 1963), one student may play Max while other students portray their individual Wild Thing. In this way, all students are participating, yet those who may be a bit reluctant will gain experience and confidence as a group player. Students in our classrooms come from a variety of ethnic, linguistic, and cultural backgrounds. This heterogeneous garden of learners may find expression for their values, thoughts, ideas, and feelings through story dramatization. When children experience a story through dramatic action and then relate that expression to literacy, both interpretative and expressive language skills are expanding (Cecil, & Lauritzen, 1994).

The most effective approach to character selection—who will play which role—begins with students choosing the characters they would like to play. We encourage students to choose more than one character to ensure they will have a choice. Several students may select a more popular character as their first choice. Naturally, not all will be able to play the main characters; however, during warm-up students will have occasions to be a favorite character although they may not play that role in the story dramatization. It is more effective to select the favorite characters first. If students are not cast in their first choice, they will have opportunities to play another role. Once again, the teacher is the encouraging force to ensure that all students are willing to play other roles. This can be accomplished by stressing that *all* roles are important to the dramatic playing. In *Katie's Trunk* (Turner, 1992) Katie is a primary character, while her brother and sister are minor characters. Yet they are key characters in creating Katie's family for whom she is willing to take great risks. Teacher attitude is the *big* variable when getting students to agree to play roles other than the lead. When there is a student who can't see the importance of all the story's characters and will play *only* the lead, J. Daniel uses a strategy that has the student watch the dramatization. This offers the student an opportunity to appreciate the importance of each character. J. Daniel dialogues with all students illustrating the importance of each character. He then asks the one student who refused to participate to play a role. We find this approach to be successful with students learning that there are no small parts in a story dramatization.

The teacher then assigns students to the different roles. This first playing is a balanced casting to ensure the story dramatization will bring together a mixture of students. This would include mixing students who are eager and comfortable with play acting with students who tend to be watchers rather than doers. This balancing ensures that different playings of the story are equally successful and interesting to all students.

Organizing the playing begins with identifying which scenes will be played, which characters will be present, and how the action will be portrayed. If the storybook is episodic or a chapter book, it may be preferable to play the story in segments. This makes the story dramatization move along with greater student understanding and involvement. An additional perk is the variety of opportunities for each child to have a chance to be a part of the story playing.

It is integral to the dramatization to talk with students about the importance of remaining in character throughout the action of the improvised play. In other words, you act as the character, you move like the character, you talk like the character, you *are* the character.

First Playing

As the first playing begins it is worthwhile to remind the students to stay in character as they act out the story. At all times during the dramatization it should be the *characters* we see and hear, not the students in the classroom. The teacher, unless the playing is completely off-track, should not interfere or correct the students during the playing. Students are encouraged to think about who they are during the playing to assure that their character's reactions, dialogue, and physical movements are true to the content of the story. When students think of this as their responsibility, it makes the story progress more smoothly with students experiencing a greater feeling of accomplishment.

The first playing may not be exactly what you picture in your mind; the first attempts at classroom dramatization may often leave a teacher feeling disappointed. This may be due to the students' becoming more interested in the props than in the story's interpretation. (Yet this beginning is natural to all of life's activities.) It is with continuing efforts that drama will become a free-flowing classroom activity. We find that the disappointing dramatization is considered just that—a door to examining what went right and where the action went wrong. The initial efforts in any kind of activity may be compared to learning how to make fish soup. It is by adding varying ingredients in varying amounts, then tasting, adapting, and experimenting that a bouillabaisse is created. The best story dramatizations result from repeated experiences. Students eager to express their ideas discover it may be hard to express what they have in mind, or they realize that although the idea is a good one, it would be impossible to dramatize. One of the main objectives of story playing is to allow students to assess and reevaluate their work as a group. Through repeated practice, they become aware of how to evaluate each of their playings. This act of considering initiates a reflective tone leading to modifying future playings. Students become aware of how to evaluate as they talk through a playing and convey a willingness to do it again, incorporating ideas to strengthen the playing. Our classroom adventures have given us numerous chances to experience story dramatization as a process in which learning is the thinking about and talking through the playing and then moving on to other dramatic interpretations.

Evaluation of the Playing

Evaluating a story dramatization is an essential component of the drama-as-learning cycle. If students do not stop and appraise the dramatic event before moving to subsequent activities, the value of story dramatization is diminished. The purpose of evaluating a dramatization is for students to learn how to self-assess. Self-assessment offers students a close look at how they might use varying dramatic techniques as well as a chance to delve into their personal connection to the story. This exploration into the dramatic event fosters participation among the students as a means to consider alternative ways to doing and being. The evaluation is not a critical analysis but rather a means to consider alternatives, other ways of doing—there are no absolutes in drama-literature instruction.

Primary points to address in a story dramatization evaluation include:

1. **Story**
   - Did the played scenes tell the storyline clearly?
   - If someone did not know the story, would they know what was taking place?
   - Are there scenes to be taken out or added to the next playing?

2. **Characterization**
   - Were the characters portrayed in keeping with the story?
   - Were the characters authentic?
   - Did the students remain in role as their character throughout the playing?

3. **Action**
   - Did the physical actions students chose to perform present the story in a realistic fashion?
   - Was there a balance between physical action and verbal response? Too much action for the dramatization? Too much talking, with no action, in the dramatization?
   - If there was too much action, what should be taken out? If the scenes don't seem to move along, what might be added to increase "physicalization"?

4. **Dialogue**
   - Was the students' improvised talking congruent with the character and the story?
   - Did the dialogue stay on track with the storyline without rambling about other subjects?
   - Were there subjects that the characters needed to talk about but were not included or addressed?
   - Did the dialogue carry the story? If not, what changes could be made to bring the action and dialogue into agreement?

5. **Timing**
   - Were the flow and portrayal of the story in sync?
   - Was the playing too rushed or did it drag?
   - How might the rhythm of the dramatization be changed for different moods or effects?

6. **Teamwork**
   - How did the students respond to each other?
   - Did students listen to the other characters and then respond in character?
   - Where did the characters work as a whole?

- If all the students were animal characters from *The Wind in the Willows* (Grahame, 1908), did they seem like animals?

7. **Enunciation and Projection**
   - Were we all able to hear the characters speaking?
   - Could you understand what was being said?
   - Were the different vocal expressions such as sounds of laughter, coughing, and sighing articulated clearly and for a reason?

8. **Natural Occurrences** (These are not evaluated.)
   - A character says the wrong line by accident.
   - A student forgets where the imaginary door is located for entering and leaving the playing space.
   - Characters forget to use an imaginary prop or that they are using one. An example would be a character drinking a glass of water and then never setting the glass down; it seems to just disappear out of the character's hand.

The fundamental idea to evaluating a story dramatization is the offering of choice. Students consider the first story playing and then consider the different possibilities that may extend and enrich subsequent playings.

Second Playing

A second playing should, by its very nature, be different from the first playing. Different students may be playing the roles; therefore, new character interpretations will occur. Even if the casting does not change, the second playing should reflect suggestions made during the evaluation, with specific focus given to those ideas that will improve the story dramatization. All of the students should have had a chance to get their feet wet during the warm-up and first playing, so the players in the second dramatization tend to exhibit more confidence in their role playing. It is important for teachers to encourage the students to try out new and interesting ideas during the second playing because at times students are content to rehash what was improvised in previous playings. If the second playing seems to need a bit of spicing up, the teacher may enter the improvisation as a character to stir things up. This teacher-in-role technique (see Chapter 3 for details regarding teacher-in-role) can provide a method for introducing new ideas into the playing without stopping the action and discussing how to change the story dramatization. Teacher-in-role also requires the students to exhibit higher-level improvisation skills — thinking on their feet. The teacher can also provide a different course of action and provide a gentle, guiding hand to those students who may not be able to concentrate. This can prompt the students to use their imaginations and perhaps become new characters or elevate their level of involvement.

Story Drama Session 1: *A Time of Angels* (Hesse, 1995)

I. This historical fiction portrays the story of a young protagonist, Hannah, who lives in a crowded tenement in Boston's West End during 1918. A deadly influenza epidemic strikes and Hannah's family is torn apart. Her younger sisters die and Hannah is guided by a vision of a girl with violet eyes away from the Boston epidemic.

Students read the book independently. The teacher may wish to select specific chapter to read aloud which may become the focus for a session. Such an example might be Chapter 4, which describes how public institutions were closed to prevent the spread of influenza.

II. Students and teacher discuss story's characters and how their characterization develops. The primary characters—Uncle Klaus, Hannah, and Tanta Rose—are developed with strong characterization by the author. With the teacher initiating character discussions, questions might include: (1) Are the characters believable? (2) Are there characters who have particular traits or behaviors? How do these define the character? (3) What are the students' special story characters and segments? (4) What role does a character play in a story?

The teacher, following the discussion, invites students to select a story character to develop in a character walk. This character walk asks students, through dramatization, to portray a specific activity of their character.

III. Planning

Students are divided into pairs. Each pair selects a two-person angel scene to create an enactment. An angel scene is a story segment where one might imagine an angel being present. The enactment portrays the angel as if it had a hand in the outcome of the action. Students work in different areas of the classroom as they select, review, and rehearse their self-selected scenes. When pairs are ready to begin playing their angel scenes, one area is selected as the playing area in which each pair will share their work with the class.

IV. First Playing

The student pairs will play the scences according to the plot sequence. The teacher organizes the pairs prior to the playing. The teacher simply asks which scene comes first, second, and so on.

(continued on page 50)

This ordering of the playing creates a smooth transition from one pair to the next. Additionally, this dialogue provides a natural backdrop to discussing the story further. The teacher's organizing the playing is essential to classroom dramatic action.

V. Evaluation

After the first playing the teacher and students discuss the sharing of the different angel scenes. Questions to focus the group discussion might include:

- Were there particular actions someone performed that seemed very true to their character? (If the same character was played in different playings, encourage students to consider how the different portrayals varied.)
- Were there characters you understood better after seeing them speak and move? If so, what became more apparent? How did this develop?
- Each pair discusses which changes they would make if given the chance to play the scene a second time. Ideas may be shared within a larger group.

VI. Second playing

Students have an opportunity to play a different character. Switching roles encourages students to consider a different perspective of the character(s). Characterization—getting inside a character—is the instructional objective in angel scene playing. The second playing would involve the pairs either switching roles or changing partners. This gives each student an opportunity to play two characters.

Story Drama Session 2: *Heroes* (Mochizuki, 1995)

I. Presenting the Story

The teacher reads *Heroes* aloud to the students. Reading aloud brings together the learning of language through physical action, and is one the most effective instructional approaches any teacher has to use.

II. Story Discussion and Warm-up

Students and teacher discuss what characteristics make a person a hero. Questions might include: Why do you think Donnie's uncle says a real hero doesn't brag? What traits do you think a hero possesses? How do you interpret Donnie's father and uncle coming to school in their uniforms?

The teacher, following the discussion, divides students into small groups of six. A warm-up activity involves each group creating a scene where one person is made fun of by the rest of the group. The teacher may have the groups share these scenes either as an improvisation or through discussion. If improvisation is the tool for sharing, the teacher may need to remind students they are role playing. The teacher encourages a setting where students respect each other's feelings.

III. Planning

Students remain in their small groups and prepare a dramatization of *Heroes*.

Teacher and students begin by outlining on the blackboard the plot summary of the story. This summary will be helpful during the groups' preparation. The groups then begin to develop their own dramatic intepretation. If classroom space is large enough, it may be preferable for each group to have their own playing space to rehearse and then subsequently share their dramatization.

IV. First Playing

The groups, when each is prepared, share their dramatization of *Heroes* before the large group. The dramatic presentations are organized to provide a structure for which group is first, second, and so on. If time is given to basic organizational strategies, the playings will encourage students to actively create their knowing by doing.

An alternate approach to planning and playing *Heroes* would be to assign a specific scene from the book to each group. The playing is then presented in sequential order according to the book.

V. Evaluation

Evaluating/discussing the playing of *Heroes* is a critical part of the dramatic action. We find that students are willing to reflect on their dramatic experiences and are easily prompted by open-ended questions. Types of questions could include:
- If you played the role of Donnie, what emotions did you feel as the character? Was there a particular reason you felt these emotions?

(continued on page 52)

- If you played the role of one of the other kids in the story, how did it feel to play this type of role where you are making fun of someone? (Whatever the answer, ask why those feelings were associated with a particular character.)
- What parts of this story and dramatization have you experienced or witnessed in your own life?
- Allow small groups to discuss what changes they might make for the second playing.

VI. Second Playing

There are three options for a second playing of *Heroes.* The first is a playing (replaying) with the cast from the first playing remaining in their character but incorporating any new ideas they may have developed. The second option is for the group members to change roles within their groups. Another possibility is for the second playing to build off the warm-ups, with each group creating and dramatizing its own hero stories.

**Story Drama Session 3: *Spin a Soft Black Song*
(Giovanni, 1971), *Confetti: Poems for Children*
(Mora, 1996), and *Nathaniel Talking* (Greenfield, 1988).**

I. Presenting the Story

Students individually select a poetry book to read during free-choice reading time. Over a week's time they would have opportunities to read the poetry book. The teacher may want to do some oral reading of different poems to show students how a poem reads.

II. Story Discussion and Warm-up

The warm-up for the dramatization provides time and opportunity for each student to read their favorite poem aloud to the class. It may be useful to have students work in pairs to prepare their oral poetry readings. There is no cause for alarm if several students select the same poem. Simply allow each student to read aloud. We find that each reading is as unique as the students themselves.

Students share their favorite poems and then as a large group discuss their readings. A teacher may initiate student discussion with these questions: How are poems different from narrative stories? Do poems tell stories? Were there any themes that seemed similar among the various poems that were read aloud?

III. Planning

The whole group selects one poem to use as an example for the first playing in this poetry dramatization session. Once the poem is selected, teacher and students create an improvised playing complete with dialogue. The playing is grounded in the students' intepretation of the poem.

The teacher will want to write the improvised play on the blackboard or overhead. This recording should be in complete form with stage directions and dialogue. It is productive to show students examples of a script in order for them to understand the writing style and technique.

The writing is actually the adapting of the poem into a play. This first writing is a demonstration of playwriting techniques. This direct instruction may involve much student and teacher dialogue as students become familiar with playwriting. When the adapting of the poem is complete, students will need to decide where and how the poem will be played.

IV. First Playing

The teacher will provide opportunities for several groups of students to act out the poem. These playings give as many students as possible the chance to act out the same piece and allows everyone to participate and build on each other's ideas.

V. Evaluation

Evaluation of the playing is the final stage of dramatization. The teacher uses an open-ended setting where students are free to share their feelings. This attitude of accepting all students' responses is essential if drama is to provide a way for students to learn.

Questions to generate the discussion:

- How do poems and plays differ from one another?
- What do poems and plays have in common?

(continued on page 54)

- Did the dialogue add to the meaning of the poem when it was turned into a play? In what way?
- What elements of the poem were most helpful in creating the play?
- Playwrights usually do some revisions after they hear their plays read by actors for the first time. If we do the same, are there any changes to be made in the script that might make it more effective?

VI. Second Playing

The teacher divides the class into small groups. Each group is asked to choose a poem from one of the poetry texts and develop it into an improvised play (story dramatization) complete with dialogue and action.

Concluding Thoughts

Keeping it real is the keystone of story dramatization. When story enactment builds on experiences where students provide the primary action, they have an opportunity to act out their learning.

Improvisation builds on the content of the story. The students are encouraged to live the story as the characters. This opportunity to walk in the shoes of the characters will nudge students to portray characters as genuine and sincere. Additionally, this focus on the characters' realism will move the student from overacting and making a game of story dramatization. The students are the characters and not caricatures.

Teachers faithfully need to stimulate the students toward using their imaginations. It is important to remember that informal, improvised story dramatization is *not* intended for an audience. Never emphasize the playing as a formal production, but rather as a sharing. It is fine to have the students share their dramatizations with other students, but let this happen naturally. In other words, when the students are ready to share with others they will let you know. *Remember:* the real purpose of a story dramatization is that students gain from the whole experience. Simply stated, the goals of story dramatization are: (1) students exhibit independent thinking, (2) students learn to view the world from someone else's perspective, (3) students undergo the experience as a team player, and (4) students experience a real-world emotional release.

By letting go of a need for perfection in the students' story dramatization, teachers will come to understand how story enactment creates an experience where learning centers around active participation. Story dramatization creates opportunities for learners to make choices, play those choices, and then consider the effect of those choices. Story dramatization is learning in action.

References

Cecil, Nancy L., and Phyllis Lauritzen. 1994. *Literacy and the Arts for the Integrated Classroom: Alternative Ways of Knowing*. New York: Longman.

Dahl, Roald. 1988. *James and the Giant Peach*. New York: Puffin Books.

Hesse, Karen. 1995. *A Time of Angels*. New York: Hyperion Paperbacks for Children.

Mochizuki, Ken. 1995. *Heroes*. New York: Lee and Low Books.

Polacco, Patricia. 1994. *Pink and Say*. New York: Philomel Books.

Sendak, Maurice. 1963. *Where the Wild Things Are*. New York: HarperCollins.

Stevenson, Robert Louis. 1883. *Treasure Island*. New York: Penguin Books.

Sims, Radine. 1977. "Reading Literature Aloud." In *Literature and Young Children*. B. E. Cullinan and C. W. Carmichael (Eds.). Urbana, IL: National Council of Teachers of English.

Turner, Ann. 1992. *Katie's Trunk*. New York: Macmillan.

Twain, Mark. 1876. *The Adventures of Tom Sawyer*.

Ward, Winifred. 1952. *Stories to Dramatize*. New Orleans: Anchorage Press.

Note

1. We have been greatly influenced by Winifred Ward's early work with story dramatization. Although every teacher using drama in a classroom develops her own style, Ward's basic methods remain influential today. Along with other teachers and children, we thank Winifred Ward for pioneering drama in education.

5
Organizing Curriculum Around Dramatic Playings: Language Arts

"... reading, like all natural gifts, must be nourished ... you nourish it, in much the same way you nourish the gift of writing—you read, think, talk, look, listen, hate, fear, love, weep—and bring your life to what you read."

KATHERINE PATERSON, 1990

Focus Questions **What role can drama play in literacy development? Just how might drama fit within the language arts curriculum?**

A Close-Up of Drama

Students in Mrs. Lewis's reading/writing workshop have selected death and dying as themes to direct their inquiry study. They have selected a storybook and formed literature study groups. The primary reading texts are *Charlotte's Web* (White, 1952), *Bridge to Terabithia* (Paterson, 1977), and *Missing May* (Rylant, 1992). Each group has selected a story scene to interpret dramatically. The groups are to pick a scene where the protagonist is dealing with death in some way. The *Missing May* group picks the scene where Ob is recounting, to Summer, memories of May. The *Bridge to Terabithia* group selects the scene where Jesse's daddy is discussing Leslie's death as an attempt to help him understand. And the *Charlotte's Web* group identifies the scene where Charlotte is telling Wilbur that she is dying and that he will need to care for her egg sac until her offspring are born. Following each group's dramatic playing, students write in their reading logs a personal re-

56

sponse to how each distinct storybook character reacts differently to death in varying situations.

This language arts lesson exemplifies drama as a teaching/learning process in a language arts curriculum. Dramatic action, when woven throughout literature studies, becomes a way to learn. This process breathes life into both writing and reading as students create literary dramatic representations. Drama offers one of the more accessible avenues to literature because it is composed of verbal action which requires students to think and react (Moffet, 1968). Dramatizing literature, as a way to read, also offers students an opening to reflective thinking with a whole range of possibilities to develop language arts instruction. This instructional process encourages students to extend their understanding through meaningful action. Students, asked to choose passages from *Out of the Dust* (Hesse, 1997) and to create a choral dramatization, vicariously experience Billie Jo's struggles portrayed in the storybook. This choral dramatization involves students in thinking critically as they decide which passages to include in their presentation. They are also learning group cooperation as they talk with one another. Students' drama blends both reading and writing to allow for an authentic context where theme and ultimately meaning, are studied.

Working with students who are reading in book study clubs, we build language arts curriculum around dramatic experience where the surface structures of language is learned through personal experience. Ritual is a touchstone for a dramatic intepretation of Odell's *Island of the Blue Dolphins*. Student book groups select a storybook scene which represents a ritual or routine in Karana's daily life. Students write an improvisation for their group performance. These improvisations are rehearsed and performed as a whole group with background music accompanying the playing. This type of storybook enactment, which builds on the techniques of drama—voice, movement, and interpretation—becomes fundamental to literacy instruction where comprehension evolves from multiple perspectives. Drama provides learners with a natural setting where personal experience is primary to their problem solving and decision making. Use of dramatic action provides all students with abundant occasions to learn. Bringing together drama, reading, and writing enables learners to delve into an integrated curriculum where content is studied as processes and skills are refined. A reading of *Pink and Say* (Palacco, 1994) becomes language arts instruction as students assume the character of either Pink or Say and write a letter to the other friend. This writing enables students to bring their personal feelings to the writing process as they study the Civil War.

Language fluency will more likely happen when students actively engage with the content and have some degree of ownership of the learning activities (Atwell, 1987; Weaver, 1994; Calkins, 1994; Farris, 1997). Viewing students as they re-create a scene from a storybook, one notices how drama brings to life reading about sensitive topics—actually all topics. This dramatic approach to "languaging" allows students to consider their views about the topic through authentic instruction. Students studying the Vietnam War read *The Wall* (Bunting, 1990). They, after reading the storybook, drafted scripted scenes set at the Vietnam Veterans' Memorial. These scenes depict families, friends, strangers, or survivors reacting to the war and its effects on their lives. This poignant literary portrayal, merged with dramatic response, illuminates how a war and its aftermath affected lives then and now.

The language arts teacher, to meet students' developmental needs, focuses instruction on process—learning to read and write by reading and writing. This curricular design creates a context where students, along with their teacher, engage in authentic acts of reading, writing, speaking, and listening. Drama, like reading and writing, is a process where students are able to extend their language skills: group communication and cooperation, storybook intepretation, problem solving, critical thinking, and decision making.

A workshop approach, in which students learn by doing, is the critical variable in designing dramatic language arts instruction. The workshop immerses learners in (1) regular chunks of time to read and write, (2) individual selection of reading materials and writing topics, and (3) purposeful talk with their classmates and teacher (Atwell, 1987). As students perceive reading and writing as a whole, sense-making process, they are able to move deeply within the pages of a book where intense involvement, pleasure, and appreciation pave the way to reading as a writer and writing as a reader. Drama is action—reading and writing in the present. This action functions as a frame of reference for students and teacher to think together and act out the writing of reading and reading of writing.

Reading Through Drama

A teacher guides learners to interact with a literary plot, character development, primary theme, and language usage through dramatic analysis. To read a novel through dramatic interpretation allows students to live the life within the storybook. This living relationship encourages a practical approach to comprehension. Students work with interpreting a text, poem, and prose by walking dramatically through the literary events to experience firsthand the story action.

Reading requires a reader to construct meaning grounded on an inter-action with a text. Making sense of the written word is dependent on a reader's understanding the purposes for, strategies of, and context for the reading (Kletzien & Hushion, 1992). Students, as they read, may know how to do basic reading, yet are unable to apply higher-level thinking and analytical skills to materials they read (National Assessment of Educational Progress, 1984). A reader must first be able to interact with their reading, then integrate these ideas with information known, compare it to other situations, and weigh it (Rosenblatt, 1937).

Dramatic activities provide students with a genuine way to expand their interaction with a language arts curriculum where the processes of language are interrelated. This instruction uses dialogical thinking (Bakhtin, 1981), in which students are talking, listening, writing, and reading—"languaging" as a way to interpret and use language. One example of this interrelated language instruction is in a classroom where students were reading *Romeo and Juliet* (Shakespeare). They first discuss the what (action) of a student-chosen scene and then re-create the scene as a modern-day interpretation. This provides students with an example of how language changes over time. Shakespeare's Elizabethan language and students' contemporary language offer students a comparative study of the relationship between the meaning of words (deep structure) and word usage (surface structure). This lesson, at its core, uses language to study language. No student should be asked to learn a language without having multiple opportunities to use it.

Students tell us they don't understand what they are reading and that writing is boring. Drama is an instructional approach that allows students to synthesize intangible concepts while "languaging" on personal experiences. These occasions to read through dramatic action provide opportunities to examine impressions through personal involvement. This allows for greater motivation as well as participation as they produce both the processes of language and content (Anglin & Sargent, 1994). As teachers, we must be cognizant of our students' reality—what they think is important and personally valuable to them—if we are to connect them with the art of learning.

Students may be puzzled by a piece of literature, especially with the first reading. We often assume that our students will get it quicker than is often the case. Literature discussions or study guides are a mere act of introducing the storybook and are just the beginning to living the novel.

Dramatic reading instruction centers on students portraying their reading: (1) acting out character interpretations, (2) illustrating textual descriptions, (3) converting narrative into dialogue, and (4) comparing and contrasting story action with word usage. The acting of reading promotes improved comprehension, since the reading experience is one of active participation.

Not only are the students reading the text, they are rereading with a focus on interpretating what they have gleaned from the story.

Drama makes reading spring to life as the pages of the book are read through the dramatic action. The book, *Nothing But the Truth* (Avi, 1991), is structured with many narrative diary/journal-type passages that transfer

---

Language Arts Lesson 1

Nothing but the Truth (Avi, 1991).   In this powerful documentary novel, Avi examines the lines of truth, rights, rules, and responsibilities. Miscommunication and misunderstanding contribute to a story in which all the characters experience loss, and none escapes blame for the outcome.

Instructional Session

   I. Topic: Distinguishing between fact and fiction

  II. Issues of Exploration

   • Comparing narrative and dramatic text
   • Recognizing components of narrative writing
   • Knowing components of dramatic writing
   • Interpreting narrative/dramatic text

 III. Focusing Questions

   • Do you tell your parents the same story you tell yourself?
   • What factors cause you to tell the truth or not?

 IV. Planning

   • Groups of students will enact their version of a script developed from the text.
   • Divide the class into teams with four members each. Provide team members with a copy of the script (see the Philip script on page 61).
   • One member role-plays the mother, one the father, and the other two, Philip. One Philip writes and speaks the diary entries while the other acts out the improvised scenes.

  V. Playing

   • Provide rehearsal time.
   • Each team shares their narrative and dramatic interpretation of the scene.

Philip Script

From the diary of Philip Malloy, written at 10:40 P.M.

(Philip writes and speaks) Folks, got my grades. Ma asked me a few things about them before supper. I didn't say much.

(Scene is played)

(Philip writes and speaks) Then, afterward, Dad talked to me. About the grades. Wasn't that he blew his stack or anything. I told him the truth. He seemed to understand.

(Scene is played)

(Philip writes and speaks) But then he asked me about my being on the track team. Didn't know what to say. If I told him what happened he would have been really mad. So I just said I decided I wouldn't go for the tryouts. That got him upset.

(Scene is played)

(Philip writes and speaks) I just realized two things that make me want to puke. Track practice starts tomorrow and I'm NOT on the team. Also, I start homeroom with Narwin!!!!! Can't stand even looking at her. I have to find a way to get transferred out.

VI. Evaluation and Follow-Up

- Lead a discussion that focuses on when, where, and why an individual tells the truth.
- Compare and contrast the narrative and the dramatic elements of the scenes. Allow students to discuss and develop other scenes in which both narrative and dramatic elements are present.

nicely to dialogue and physical action. Transforming narrative to dramatic makes reading active for the students, and provides both an internal and external demonstration of reading comprehension.

Writing Through Drama

Writing, specifically drafting, often is considered a solitary, self-directed discovery process. This view focuses on individual effort rather than social interaction. Talk, in this setting, develops before and after the writing, not during. Students must rely on their own interpretation, recollection, motivation, and skill during the actual writing. Yet languaging is a natural entry into writing. Britton (1970) states "writing floats on a sea of talk." Drama, woven within writing instruction, blends both vocal and physical language to support students' writing development.

Drama underscores the relationship between thinking and the social organization of instruction. This student-in-social activity (Minick, 1985) places the learner with others as they create social contexts, zones of proximal development (Vygotsky, 1978), where instruction supports evolving language fluency. The teacher, through collaborating, directing, and demonstrating, guides developing writers to become aware of the author's craft through dramatic analysis of their readings. Teasing apart students' writing through dramatic interpretation allows writers to consider differing writing strategies. This translating process builds on portraying what we are writing; acting out interpretations of characters; illustrating how to utilize descriptions or dialogue to influence readers through action; and establishing word accuracy. Students, through dramatization, become aware of not only the writer's crafting strategies but also are encouraged to develop their own approach. Ultimately, this insight leads them to incorporate a variety of different techniques as a part of their writing.

Students are able to explore writing while trying on social experiences (Smith and Herring, 1993). Drama as process instruction places learners in a variety of contexts—situations where they are able to play with different forms of thought, feeling, and language. Dramatic action, within a workshop instructional setting, puts students into other people's shoes (Heathcote, 1984) by using personal experiences to help them meet firsthand the art of capturing the reader via the crafting of their writing.

Students writing can play a dual role within a dramatic language arts curriculum. One role that writing can assume is as a follow-up to the reading of a storybook. This written response may be a reaction to the story and dramatic activities. It may entail writing (1) a letter in character, (2) a descriptive essay about story setting—place and time, (3) a character journal entries, (4) a personal narrative on the theme, and (5) a newspaper article reporting the issues of the story.

A second role students' writing may play in language arts instruction is that of providing the structure to organize a dramatic playing. This may include (1) a narrative scenario outlining the who, what, when, and where, (2) a short play using dialogue and stage directions, (3) a first-person monologue, (4) a two-person scripted scene telling the story using dialogue, or (5) a written narrative pantomime using physical movement to tell the story.

Perspective is pivotal to a piece of writing. To develop the skill of identifying and developing a perspective, writers need opportunities to interact with literature, which portrays the role that perspective plays in a written

Language Arts Lesson 2

Bull Run *(Fleischman, 1993)* is a fictional tour de force that re-creates the first battle of the Civil War from sixteen points of view: Northern and Southern, male and female, white and black. Each voice—perspective—narrates the glory, grim reality, hopes, horror, and folly of discovering the genuine nature of war. This text provides a natural opportunity for the language arts teacher to show the role of point of view in writing.

Instructional Session

I. Topic: Investigating the relationship between the interpretation of an event from differing points of view

II. Issues of Exploration
   - Character sketch
   - Subject analysis inside out
   - Voice development
   - Elements of perspective

III. Focusing Questions
   - How is understanding related to perspective? How does a character's voice develop the setting and action?
   - What is the "match" between your inner and outer voice?

IV. Planning
   - Each student, after reading *Bull Run,* selects a favorite character passage. This passage serves as the material to develop a character monologue collage.
   - Monologue development directions include: (1) create a physical action such as Charlette King scrubbing clothes, Toby Boyce playing a fife, or Williane Rye doctoring. Encourage students to choose the character's physical activity based on the text; and (2) consider the vocal attitude and tone of the character as if telling their perspective (chosen passage) out loud.
   - Groups of 5 or 6 students are organized. Group composition should provide for a variety of perspectives.
   - A group storytelling performance will combine individual character monologues into a collage. Members of the group will invent a vocal refrain, such as "North, South, North, South," to link the monologues.

(continued on page 64)

- In conjunction with the repeating refrain, characters portray themselves by repeating their physical action for performance.
- The refrain and characters' physical action initiates the performance piece, serves as transition between monologues, and provides an ending.

V. Playing

- Groups are given time to prepare and rehearse their monologue performance. During this work time, the teacher moves among the groups to prompt students to fully develop their character collage by incorporating a variety of physical placements in the space. For example, characters may best be portrayed through sitting, kneeling, or reclining while others may stand. Also, characters are frozen during individual character monologue presentations.
- Each group presents its monologue collage.

VI. Evaluation and Follow-up

- Students individually brainstorm on paper a list of images that captures their character. These include color, texture, shape, taste, odor, animal, sound, and visual image.
- As a large group, discuss how the different images help to "show" character traits as well as how we "see" a character when described through the techniques of analogy, metaphor, or simile.
- From this, students are invited to compose a written narrative character description.
- The written narratives may be shared. Additionally, they will be added to the writing workshop folder.

piece. The following language arts lesson uses *Bull Run* (Fleischman, 1993) to amplify the concept of point of view. An awareness and understanding of perspective, that is, character voice, illustrates the relationship between how they view an event and the feelings associated with that event.

The Dramatic Minilesson

Drama is a stage from which to view the unfolding match between a writer's intent and the audience's interpretation. A dramatic minilesson builds on (1) writing that develops into a dramatization, and (2) improvising action that launches writing. This hands-on process to teach the craft of writing can develop through techniques such as scripting, role playing, monologue, staging, or dialogue.

We, in our classroom experiences, initiate a dramatic writing minilesson by first selecting a writer's technique—for example, fictionalizing a personal experience. We then tie the technique to the students' reading. Within the context of reading *Words by Heart* (Sebestyen, 1979), seventh graders were able to experience how to use personal experience as a base to heighten a fictional situation. Sebestyen's novel scrutinizes racial prejudices, race relationships, and nonviolence in the cotton country of the early 1900s. Lena, the young black protagonist in a church competition, recites the most scriptures by heart. Yet winning does not bring her the joy nor the recognition she had expected.

We organized an instructional episode on students' reading of Sebestyen's story by asking them to think of a personal experience of striving for a goal, which involved significant time and effort in order to achieve. Then we guided students from this reflective experience to develop a dramatic scene.

After identifying the learning outcome—writing by the creation of improvisations based on personal experience (National Standards for Arts Education, 1994)—we initiated an instructional episode based on a discussion of Lena's experience. From this group think, students wrote a brief description recalling a life event where imagined expectations and actual events match. Next, students were divided into small groups to share their writings. Then each group chose one experience involving bias, discrimination, or prejudice to add fictional circumstances to. Students then improvised scenes (acting out a situation or event with no rehearsal) of this fictionalized experience, to the larger student group. Students as a natural follow-up to this walking in the character's shoes lesson, discussed how the role playing helped to identify the link between nonfiction and fiction within one piece of writing. An example of this lesson is outlined in Figure 5–1.

Additional Dramatic Writing Minilessons

In this section are additional minilessons that connect the reading of literature to writing instruction. They reflect our teaching experiences with students in a reading/writing workshop. Using *Autumn Street* (Lowry, 1980) as the point of departure to explore voice, students investigate how a writer creates aliveness in their words (Figure 5–2). Voice is how an author portrays thought and feeling. And it is this tone in writing that ultimately creates lively, distinctive expression.

Lowry's text portrays Charles's and Elizabeth's friendship. The setting for this special relationship is the 1940s in a provincial neighborhood where Elizabeth has come to live in her grandfather's home while her father fights in World War II. Charles is the grandson of Tatie, the house cook. This

---

Dramatic Writing Minilesson 1: *Words by Heart* (Sebestyen, 1979)

Topic: Fictionalizing a personal experience

Objective: Explore how to link nonfiction and fiction in a piece of writing

Culminating Event: Students perform improvised scenarios of a fiction-alized experience

Learning Outcome: Writing a narrative as explored through the impro-visations of a personal experience

Process/Procedure

- Begin minilesson with a discussion to interpret Lena's experi-ence in the contest.
- Follow up this group talk by writing a brief description of an event from the students' life experiences where imagined ex-pectations and actual events match.
- Share written events; divide students into small groups.
- Direct small groups to choose one shared experience to add fictional circumstances to involving bias, discrimination, or prejudice.
- Create a small-group improvised scene of the fictionalized event (7 to 10 minutes). If time permits, scenes can be shared with the larger group.
- Engage students in a talk-back regarding role playing the scenes as a means to identify and discuss how to link nonfiction and fiction within one context.

Figure 5–1. *Words by Heart*

emotionally charged story presents a dilemma where Elizabeth's extended family examines the layers of friendship in a separate and not equal world.

Lowry's memorable writing can be savored and weighed. In one instance, students were asked to consider the following passage. "For days there was a haze in the room, so that everything was veiled; but the haze seemed to be be-hind my own eyes, deep in the hot part of my head, where something ached and throbbed with the same rhythm as my pulse."(p. 178). This sentence, through metaphor and imagery, is saying, "I am sick," and is an example of how an au-thor creatively uses words to paint pictures. Through discussion, students handled the writer's crafting.

Students often have difficulty capturing voice in their writing (Lane, 1993) primarily as a result of few opportunities to express, through speaking

---

Dramatic Writing Minilesson 2: *Autumn Street* (Lowry, 1980)

Topic: Voice (lively, distinctive expression)

Objective: Examine the concept of voice in writing

Culminating Event: Students write, using the perspective of a character from student-developed improvisations

Learning Outcome: Writing with voice by speaking/interacting in improvised scenes

Process/Procedure

- Divide students into pairs. One portrays Elizabeth and the other, Charles.
- Initiate minilesson with the teacher saying, "Create a scene in which Charles appears to Elizabeth during one of her feverish nightmares. Develop a dialogue/conversation between the two where they talk about their friendship and the events surrounding the last time they were together."
- Pair students to play this scene (5 to 7 minutes).
- Talk with students to view feelings, thoughts, and meaning attached to the characters' spoken dialogue. This interchange should attempt to analyze how feelings and meaning change as they move from an oral to written form. This examination of voice may last 7 to 10 minutes and builds from students' improvisations.
- Invite students to develop a "voice" for a self-selected character who expresses their innermost feelings regarding another situation or person. The writing genre also is left to the students and may include poetry, a letter, a script, prose, or a journal entry.

Figure 5–2. *Autumn Street*

or writing, their beliefs or opinions on a topic. Students can meet voice when they stand on their feet and dialogue with one another in an improvised setting. This involves students in a give and take where meaning is heard through the sound of language. Hearing is the heart of writing (Kirby et al., 1981). How do we help students hear their own writing? Drama can function as an amplifier to hear the voice within their words.

Another dramatic writing minilesson (Figure 5–3) uses *The Eagle Kite* (Fox, 1995). This novel centers on thirteen-year-old Liam, who faces the challenge to accept his parents and their lifestyle choices. As a part of his

Dramatic Writing Minilesson 3: *The Eagle Kite* (Fox, 1995)

Topic: Informative discourse

Objective: Interpreting a topic

Culminating Event: Students create videotape infomercials. An info-mercial is a commercial made for the sole purpose of informing an audience about a product.

Learning Outcome: Writing to analyze methods of presentation and au-dience response

Process/Procedure

- Develop a group discussion to explore students' perception and understanding of AIDS. This information can be charted for future reference.

- Guide students to develop a group infomercial. The infomercial is to be a 30-second informative monologue. Composing is com-pleted with all students offering ideas, suggestions, and facts.

- Provide time for several students to read the infomercial monologue. These readings may be videotaped for group view-ing. This would enable the group to examine the "art" of infor-mative writing and solo speaking.

- Prompt students to self-select a topic to study and subse-quently write a 30-second infomercial. This activity may take several days as students research and analyze their topic and then proceed to compose an infomercial.

- Present students' infomercials, which have been videotaped for audience response.

Figure 5–3 *The Eagle Kite*

acceptance, Liam comes to admit that his father's illness doesn't translate into being unacceptable in or unwanted by society. One theme—seeing beyond societal bias—situates the protagonist in addressing the issues surrounding AIDS. This novel provides students with opportunities to heighten their con-ceptual understanding of expository writing through comparing, contrasting, arguing, and explaining a substantive issue.

Expository writing borrows from both narrative and descriptive writing. Literature is a natural avenue to studying exposition. Students are able to gain a sense of how this form of discourse takes shape. Exposition assumes an au-dience; yet first, a writer has to write to understand the topic. This beginning step gets the writer to focus, that is, to make sense of the subject, wrestle with ideas, and then construct lines clearly representative of those ideas (Kirby et al., 1981).

Writing helps students to explore the extent of their knowledge and perspective on a topic, as well as discover what they do and don't want to say about it. This mental engagement with a topic cannot be avoided, because writing seems to require us to organize our thoughts in some way and also to think beyond the obvious (Purves et al., 1990). The developing writer is challenged to provide more information about, more reflection on, more wrestling with the topic as they reach to write what they mean and mean what they write. Writing is a juggling act requiring the author to balance content, structure, and meaning along with perspective. If our student writers are to mature as language users, they must be able to base their writing on clear, responsible thinking. And, this in turn, requires us to organize minilessons, which support them to come up with uncluttered insights into their writing.

Another essential characteristic of good writing is the unfolding of conflict within the plot line. The plot of a story is the sequence of interrelated events linked together by causality (Russell, 1991). It is this causality, or conflict, that holds the readers' attention. A writer creates conflict in the story action when something is at stake, that is, when some difficulty must be overcome or some goal must be achieved by the protagonist. These road blocks appear as opposing forces: other characters, society, nature, self, or fate. In the novel *Dragonwings* (Yep, 1975), Moon Shadow tries to hold on to his traditional Chinese customs while making his way in San Francisco during the early 1900s. With this setting, Yep evolves the plot line through Moon Shadow's zigzagging to meet life's challenges: conflicting characters, hostile environments, shattering earthquakes, limited self-appreciation, and unpredictable events. It is this variety of just enough changing, twisting, and surprising that keeps us reading.

Children's literature spotlights conflict. And, when our instructional emphasis views literature through a dramatic lens, conflict can be magnified and subsequently studied. This situates the student writers to live conflict. An illumination of this literary element points writers in the direction of recognizing that if you ain't got conflict, you ain't got a reader. Without conflict in a piece of writing there is no building to resolution; with conflict, the reader's interest is sustained to the end (McCaslin, 1990).

Good writing has movement and order to it (Kirby et al., 1981). The writer must plan the course of events with things happening for good reason. The writing need not be a personal experience, but readers' interest will be lost if the conflict and actions are not believable. Our experiences with student writers illustrate the benefit of playing with their reading, which then leads them to recognize the power of conflict.

Dramatic Writing Minilesson 4: *Dragonwings* **(Yep, 1975)**

Topic: Conflict (the action of the story)

Objective: Comprehend the element of conflict in writing

Culminating Event: Students write a script to depict a type of conflict

Learning Outcome: The creation of conflict through writing scripted scenes

Process/Procedure

- Generate a discussion to examine the various types of conflict found in the story. These may be charted to use at a later time.
- Act out several of these moments of conflict found within the plot (5 minutes).
- Divide students into pairs.
- Direct pairs to write a script for a two-character, two-minute scene in which a self-selected issue of conflict is presented.
- Share students' scripts with a large group in the form of duet readings.

Figure 5–4.   *Dragonwings*

Concluding Thoughts

Drama is a natural process that nourishes language arts. It involves talking, listening, reading, writing, socializing, and thinking in a classroom. Teachers require tangible strategies to co-construct, with their students, a learning environment where learning becomes the doing. Our dramatic teaching experience, with learners, promotes a learning climate where their voices are heard through dramatic action. Drama, in the reading and writing workshop, casts the minilesson as a stage where the craft of writing can be seen and heard. This viewing allows instruction to be the real thing as students capture the literary life through dramatic interaction.

After reading and writing the dramatic way, our students seem to be more aware of the writer's craft as well as the mechanics and skills, which are a natural dimension of writing and reading. They become more willing to discuss from multiple perspectives their own feelings. We also notice that when instruction connects literature with dramatic interpretations a setting is created where languaging becomes the way to read and write. This dramatic twist to literacy instruction moves a learner to embrace the literate life as a means to understand self, others, and the world.

References

Anglin, J., and P. Sargent. 1994. "Nine Truths about Young Adolescent Artists." *Middle School Journal.* January, 66–68.

Atwell, Nancie. 1987. *In the Middle: Writing, Reading, and Learning with Adolescents.* Portsmouth, NH: Heinemann.

Avi. 1991. *Nothing but the Truth.* New York: Avon.

Bakhtin, Mikhail M. 1981. *Dialogic Imagination: Four Essays.* Michael Holquist (Ed.). Translated by Carly Emerson and Michael Holquist. Austin: University of Texas Press.

Beane, James A. 1992. "Turning the Floor Over: Reflections on a Middle School Curriculum." *Middle School Journal,* 34–40.

Bolton, Gavin. 1984. *Drama as Education.* New York: Longman.

Britton, James. 1970. *Language and Learning.* Coral Gables, FL: University of Miami Press.

Bunting, Eve. 1990. *The Wall.* Boston: Houghton Mifflin.

Calkins, Lucy McCormick. 1994. *The Art of Teaching Writing.* Portsmouth, NH: Heinemann.

Cooter, R. B., and G. W. Chilcoat. 1990. "Content-Focused Melodrama: Dramatic Renderings of Historical Text." *Journal of Reading* 34, 274–277.

Edmiston, Brian. 1991. "Planning for Flexibility: The Phases of a Drama Structure." *The Drama Teacher* 4, 6–11.

Farris, Pamela J. 1997. *Language Arts: Process, Product, and Assessment.* Madison, WI: Brown and Benchmark.

Faulkner, William. 1990. "Writing." In *Writers on Writing,* Jon Winokur (Ed.). Philadelphia: Running Press, 7.

Fleischman, Paul. 1993. *Bull Run.* New York: Scholastic.

Fox, Paula. 1995. *The Eagle Kite.* New York: Orchard Books.

Heathcote, Dorothy. 1984. In *Dorothy Heathcote: Collected Writings on Drama and Education.* L. Johnson and C. O'Neil (Eds.). London: Hutchinson.

Kirby, Dan, and Tom Liner, with Ruth Vinz. 1981. *Inside Out: Developmental Strategies for Teaching Writing.* Montclair, NJ: Boynton/Cook.

Kletzien, Benge S., and Conway B. Hushion. 1992. "Reading Workshop: Reading, Writing, Thinking." *Journal of Reading* 35:6, 444–451.

Lane, Barry. 1993. *After the End.* Portsmouth, NH: Heinemann.

Lasky, Kathyrn. 1994. *Beyond the Burning Time.* New York: Blue Sky Press.

Lipsyte, Robert. 1977. *One Fat Summer.* New York: HarperCollins.

Lowry, Lois. 1980. *Autumn Street.* New York: Dell Publishing.

McCaslin, Nellie. 1990. *Creative Drama in the Classroom.* New York: Longman.

Minick, N. 1985. *L. S. Vygotsky and Soviet Activity Theory: New Perspectives on the Relationship between Mind and Society.* Unpublished doctoral dissertation, Northwestern University, Evanston, IL.

Moffett, James. 1968. *Teaching the Universe of Discourse.* Boston, MA: Houghton Mifflin Company.

Moll, Lois S. 1990. Introduction. In L. S. Moll (Ed.), *Vygotsky and Education: Instructional Implications and Applications of Sociohistorical Psychology.* New York: Cambridge University Press, 1–27.

National Standards for Arts Education. 1994. *What Every Young American Should Know and Be Able to Do in the Arts.* Reston, VA: Author.

O'Dell, Scott. 1960. *Island of the Blue Dophins.* Boston: Houghton Mifflin.

Palacco, Patricia, 1994. *Pink and Say.* New York: Philomel Books.

Paterson, Katherine. 1990. How To Read. In S. Gilbar (Ed.). 1990. *The Reader's Quotation Book: A Literary Companion.* New York: Pushcart Press.

———. 1977. *Bridge to Terabithia.* New York: Thomas Y. Crowell, Publishers.

Purves, Alan C., Rogers, T. and Soter A. O. 1990. *How Porcupines Make Love II: Teaching a Response-Centered Literature Curriculum.* New York: Longman.

Rosenblatt, Louise. 1976. *Literature as Exploration.* New York: The Modern Language Association of America.

Russell, David L. 1991. *Literature for Children.* 2nd ed. New York: Longman.

Rylant, Cynthia. 1992. *Missing May.* New York: Dell Publishing.

Sebestyen, Ouida. 1979. *Words by Heart.* New York: Bantam Books.

Smith, J. Lea, and J. Daniel Herring. 1993. "Using Drama in the Classroom." *Reading Horizons* 33, 18–30.

Spinelli, Jerry. 1990. *Maniac Magee.* Boston: Little, Brown and Company.

Voight, C. 1986. *Izzy, Willy-Nilly.* New York: Fawcett Juniper.

Vygotsky, Levi S. 1978. *Mind in Society.* Cambridge, MA: Harvard University Press.

Weaver, Constance. 1994. *Reading Process and Practice: From Sociopsycholinguistics to Whole Language.* 2nd Ed. Portsmouth, NH: Heinemann.

White, E. B. 1952. *Charlotte's Web.* New York: Harper and Row.

Yep, Laurence. 1975. *Dragonwings.* New York: HarperCollins.

6
Literature and Drama: Experiencing Social Studies

"But may not literary materials contribute powerfully to student's images of the world, himself, and the human condition?"
LOUISE ROSENBLATT, 1983

Focus Question Is it possible to blend social studies curriculum, children's literature, and drama to offer students opportunities to reenact the past as a way to prepare for the future?

A Close-Up of Drama

Mr. Fulks uses *She's Wearing a Dead Bird on Her Head!* (Lasky, 1995) to involve his students in a social debate on a historical issue—the killing of animals to be used as adornment. Mr. Fulks divides his class into three groups. One group will play characters who are opposed to people wearing dead birds on their hats at the turn of the twentieth century. A second group will characterize those people who believe they have a right, if they so choose, to wear dead birds on their heads. The third group will become characters who are undecided and will be required to take a stand on this issue. Mr. Fulks plays the role of mayor of Boston. In this role, he conducts a town meeting to establish a policy regarding the wearing of dead birds on women's hats. The three groups debate, in character, the issues. The town meeting concludes, with a vote, on whether or not dead birds can be worn as hat decorations in public.

This instructional session highlights the quintessence of social studies. The social studies curriculum promotes knowledge of and involvement in civic affairs (National Council for the Social Studies, 1994). Students learn basic knowledge and ways to analyze and think. Incorporating literature and

73

dramatic action makes use of different academic disciplines by placing students in a dilemma in which they learn how to analyze their own and others' opinions on important civic issues. The students within Mr. Fulks' social studies classroom are gaining historical knowledge while becoming involved in current day social decision making.

Studying social studies can be an exciting and beneficial endeavor for all young people. Unfortunately, many students don't believe this. Their disbelief may be because they have a hard time relating to what seems to be isolated facts thrown into a textbook. What students fail to realize is that social studies is more than isolated facts. It is a reflection of the moral, social, and economic context of our past, our today, and our tomorrow. Yet, even when teachers present such a valid argument to students, they still often fail to note the relevance of social studies to their present lives.

Perhaps this argument is part of the problem of teaching and learning social studies. Instead of looking at social studies as the past—something over and done with—we need to start viewing social studies from a more personal and current perspective. Teachers need to present social studies as a human pursuit which ought to be questioned (Wineburg, 1991). And students need to use social studies curricular activities as a forum for questioning and defining their own code of ethics. Social studies is more than a product; it is a process of understanding and clarifying the continuum of human motives as they relate to individuals as well as societies and cultures at large.

We present, in this chapter, an instructional approach to the teaching of social studies that combines literature with drama to analyze the human experience.

First, we discuss the foundation of a social studies curriculum. Second, we present the organizational structure used to integrate dramatic interpretation of literature, including historical novels. Third, we suggest appropriate instructional strategies to engage students in the reflective questioning of human motives in a social context.

Social Studies Standards

The primary purpose of social studies is to help young people develop the ability to make informed and reasoned decisions for the public good as citizens of a culturally diverse, democratic society in an interdependent world. Social studies is the integrated study of the social sciences and humanities to promote civic competence. Social studies curriculum provides coordinated, systematic study drawing upon such disciplines as anthropology, archeology, economics, geography, history, law, philosophy, political science, psychology, religion, and sociology, as well as appropriate content from the humanities, mathematics, and natural sciences (National Council for the Social Studies, 1994).

The National Social Studies Standards are composed of ten primary themes, which include (1) culture; (2) time, continuity, and change; (3) people, places, and environments; (4) individual development and identity; (5) individuals, groups, and institutions; (6) power, authority, and governance; (7) production, distribution, and consumption; (8) science, technology, and society; (9) global connections; and (10) civic ideals and practices. These thematic strands are interrelated in such a way that the design of a social studies curriculum builds naturally from one theme to the next. For example, students who read and then act out scenes from *The Winter Room* (Paulsen, 1989) are able to examine and begin to understand firsthand the relationship among people, places, and environments. The story setting captures farm life in the 1920s, when our culture was more agrarian, with life revolving around the seasons. As students grasp this interactive relationship between humans and their environment, they then are able to concretely perceive how a culture is dynamic and evolving in response to change.

Building Connections Within a Social Studies Curriculum

If a social studies curriculum is to build a connection for learners, the learning and teaching occurring within the classroom must first be meaningful. What the students learn needs to be real—useful in the outside world. Real-world learning takes place as students become participants in a thorough examination, not a superficial view, of a topic. Next, social studies learning is more effective when it is integrated with other content disciplines. This integration builds knowledge and skills across disciplines as well as provides a classroom environment where multiple perspectives are encouraged. The third component of effective social studies teaching and learning is rooted in a curriculum where students and teacher consider ethical dimensions of controversial issues with a reflective concern for the common good. The issues we face in our social world involve costs and benefits—a give-and-take for differing groups of people. It is these two foci, cost and benefit, that act as the basis to examining the human condition—social studies. Students and teachers examine, reflect upon, and respect opposing viewpoints of critical societal issues.

An important aspect of social studies curriculum is the challenge to build on the art of thinking. The pivotal goal is to nurture a classroom setting where a thoughtful approach to inquiry elicits responses from students that challenge the status quo. The social studies curriculum stimulates students' thinking that is founded on well-reasoned arguments as opposed to personal opinions lacking thought and reasoning. The teacher's willingness to be open to diverse thinking is decisive. Finally, students learn social studies best when it is an active process. The social studies curriculum involves activities where real-life application of decision making and construction of knowledge unfold. The teacher is then released from being the single guiding force in instruction and hands the reins to the students as they become more independent learners.

Teaching Social Studies with Literature and Drama

In the typical social studies classroom the basic mode of instruction is the textbook. The textbook is a useful source of content information and provides a general outline and structure to key content concepts under study. Textbooks generally are designed to provide coverage of a topic quickly and efficiently, without developing any human connection with the topic. This may limit the reader from interacting with human endeavors that are the primary threads to constructing social studies curriculum. While the textbook provides the parameters of study, a wide assortment of facts and generalization, and guides teacher planning, it does not provide for an in-depth transaction between the student and the subject (Beck, McKeown, and Gromoll, 1989).

Textbooks have a role within the social studies classroom, yet because of their limitations, they should not be the only source of information for student learning. In their research of social studies textbooks, Beck et al. (1991), noted that textbooks lack the depth needed to develop an understanding of the sequence of historical events. To overcome these limitations, we recommend using historical fiction as a complementary source of content information. Historical fiction used in conjunction with the social studies textbook establishes relevancy between the student and historical events.

Just as with historical fiction, biographies, autobiographies, and contemporary realistic fiction personalize events and foster a sense of the continuity of life. Students begin to see themselves and the present as part of the living past (Huck, 1979). Literature also reflects the human condition and provides an insight into human motivations from various perspectives. When we, as teachers, present multiple perspectives of social studies by combining literature, drama, and a study of history, students develop a broader vision and a greater depth of understanding for historical and social events. Because historical novels deal with the complexity of being human, students are exposed to how history, with its human causes and effects, impacts the present.

Combining the textbook, historical fiction, and dramatic action creates an environment where students can analyze, question, and reflect on the people and events we know as social studies. Our goal is to create an environment where a transaction between the student and history occurs. This promotes a consideration of human motive and subsequent action. These interactive learning episodes generate topic coverage at various depths. From these learning episodes, students can build critical thinking skills and achieve a more intricate awareness of how history is the story of people's lives.

Social Studies Lesson 1

Nettie's Trip South (Turner, 1987). Turner's text is based on her great-grandmother's diary that recounts her reaction to slavery in pre-Civil War South.

Instructional Session

I. Topic: Exploring cultural perspectives

II. Issues of Exploration
   - Multiple perspectives of self and others
   - Issues surrounding cultural prejudices
   - Role playing

III. Focusing Questions
   - What is it like to "walk in the shoes" of someone who is different from you?
   - How does it feel to be judged by how you look?

IV. Planning
   - Divide the class into two groups on opposite sides of the room.
   - Include only one group in a brief discussion focusing on aspects of cultural prejudices while totally excluding the other group.
   - Discussion may include topics, such as how we judge others based on the choices they make: clothing, food preferences, hair style, or friends.
   - The discussion may last 5 to 7 minutes.
   - Involve the "excluded" group and ask about their perspective concerning being left out of the discussion. This exchange builds on their feelings and what it is like to be discriminated against.
   - Building on a natural point of transition, instruct students to line up in the center of the classroom.
   - Initiating the drama session, the teacher says, "I am now going to label each side of the classroom as an item. You then move to the side of the class with the label with which you most closely identify. Thus, even though you may identify with both, you will need to make a choice. After your first choice, you will remain on that side of the room. Then with the next label assignment, you may stay where you are, or move to the opposite side."

(continued on page 78)

- Below are label suggestions for the sides of the room that will provide experiences to explore and extend the earlier discussion and add to the perspective of peer pressure.

Label suggestions:

Volkswagen	Cadillac
apple	orange
steak	pizza
fork	spoon
red	blue
fish	chicken
smooth	rough
rain	snow
jeans	dress clothes
cat	dog
solids	stripes
morning	evening
scream	whisper

V. Playing

- Divide students into two groups.
- Provide each group with a descriptive narrative for only one of the cultures listed.

Culture One

Culture One people are very friendly. They never pass up an opportunity to touch others with a warm gesture; they never shake hands, though; this is not considered a warm enough gesture. Instead, they pat your shoulder or back, and perhaps give a hug.

It seems that their main interest is their family background. They love to talk about parents, siblings, even distant relations, but they would never talk about themselves; that would be too vain. They would rather tell you what they are like through whispers, not in ordinary conversational tone. But when it comes to talking about other people in their family, they'll speak with gusto and energy.

There is only one thing that insults the people of Culture One; if a member of another culture says the first word in a conversation, members of Culture One just walk away from them without saying a word. But if Culture One members get the first word in, the conversation will be pleasant and fruitful (Saldana, 1987).

Culture Two

Culture Two people are money-oriented. They constantly want to borrow money from others. Of course, they never borrow from people of their own culture; instead, they try to get it from foreigners. They wait until the "right" moment to talk about money—they always have an excellent reason for needing the money—even if the reason is not always truthful. These people are also very nosy; they love to pry into other people's lives. They want to know everything about the people from other cultures.

Whenever members of Culture Two meet anyone, the traditional greeting is lightly tapping the top of that person's right or left hand three times. Aside from that, they refrain from all other types of physical contact.

There is only one thing that insults the people of Culture Two; if anyone talks about their brothers or sisters. They regard siblings as competition for money; hence, they are insulted if anyone mentions them. Parents and other relations are a fine topic for conversation. But if someone discusses their siblings, their facial expression turns to anger, and they walk away without saying a word (Saldana, 1987).

- Encourage each group to discuss quietly their assigned culture so that the other group will not overhear. When both groups have had ample planning/discussion time, have the two cultures meet one another at some type of social function such as a party. Students are prompted to find out as much about the other culture as possible.
- Allow the improvisation to last about 5 to 7 minutes.

VI. Evaluation and Follow-Up

- Lead a discussion about the traits of each culture, as well as a broader discussion dealing with cultural differences.
- Encourage students to express their insights and feelings when they were the "outsider." Also, identify how others influence how we behave.
- Expand by creating new, improvised situations, such as a blind date between two persons (one from each culture), an elevator stuck between two floors with people from different cultures trapped together, and an all-girl or boy party in which only one member from the other gender is present.

(continued on page 80)

A second approach to social studies mixes content knowledge with extending students' process skills development through multi-cultural materials.

Social Studies Lesson 2

Shadow (Brown, 1982). Brown's text is an illustrated version of an African-inspired French poem that evokes a dancing image—Shadow. The eerie, shifting image of Shadow appears where there is light and fire and a storyteller to bring it to life.

Instructional Session

I. Topic: Story as cultural history

II. Issues of Exploration

- Multicultural literature
- Dialect
- Movement as story
- Human migration patterns

III. Focusing Questions

- What is a story? How can movement become an element of the storyline?
- In what ways does the "imaginary" build story? What is the relationship between a cultural group and their historical stories?

IV. Planning

Part One
- Divide students into pairs and then identify each student within pairs as either A or B.
- Pairs stand back to back.
- Teacher says, "Student A, decide where the sun is shining: on your front, your back, or your side. Now, step in the direction that will make your partner, student B, become your shadow. Student B, shadow all the movements of student A."
(Allow this warm-up period to last a couple of minutes. Then, have A and B switch roles.)

Part Two
- Pairs again move to stand back to back.
- Teacher says, "Student A, using the words, 'Good day, my name is . . . ,' change your voice in pitch, rhythm, tempo, or range of sound. When I say 'Go,' partners will face each other and B will shadow A's chosen vocal expression."
(Give students A and B the opportunity to create their own vocal expressions and then have them shadowed.)

Part Three
- Pairs return to stand back to back.
- Teacher says, "Student A, using the same vocal expression, think of an appropriate physical movement to accompany it. When I say, 'Go,' partners face each other. Then, B shadow A's body movements and vocal expressions."

V. Playing

- Divide the students into three groups.
- Designate groups to undertake either the vocal, the physical, or the combination playing of the passage, including both movement and voice.
- Provide each group with a copy of the passage:

> "Shadow is a fall.
> They say also
> that it is the mother
> of all that crawls,
> of all that squirms.
> For as soon as the sun comes up,
> here are the shadow people,
> breaking loose, unwinding,
> stretching, stirring,
> branching out, teeming,
> like snakes, scorpions
> and worms."
>
> *Passage from* Shadow *(Brown, 1982)*

(Allow each of the groups time to organize their playing. The time may vary, but we usually give our groups about ten minutes.)

(continued on page 82)

- During this group-work period, the teacher moves from group to group "side-coaching."
- Teacher says to the voice group, "Think of all the different ways you can use your voice to make sound effects as well as spoken words. Then, look at your passage and select lines or perhaps even just a word or words that could be read as a solo, duet, or choral reading."
- Teacher says to the physical group, "Remember, you are to perform the passage using physical actions to tell the story. You won't use your voice or sounds. You may decide as a group to act out your passage as a whole group playing with individuals performing different portions of the passage at the same time."
- Teacher says to the combination group, "You have the task of combining voice and physical action to dramatize the passage. You may wish to use random sound effects as well as spoken words with physical actions that are completed as a whole group or by individuals."
- Groups share their dramatic playing beginning with the voice group, the physical group, and then the combination group.

VI. Evaluation and Follow-Up

- Involve students in a large-group discussion.
- The teacher guides the discussion by asking, "How did you feel about having to rely on just your particular mode of communication to relate the passage to the rest of the class?" "Which mode of communication are you most comfortable using and for what reasons?" "With what kind of people and in what kind of circumstances do we find use of these different kinds of communication?"
- Allow students to respond in a give-and-take discussion that addresses other issues and topics germane to the playing.

Social Studies Lesson 3

Anne Frank: The Diary of a Young Girl (1953). This famous diary of a young writer has become a touchstone to the reality of how adolescents felt during a time in history that has been etched in our minds through the many images of concentration camps, The Star of David, and Adolf Hitler.

Instructional Session

I. Topic: Living history through story

II. Issues of Exploration

- Historical events
- Holocaust
- Debate
- Human attitudes

III. Focusing Questions

- How is history told through story?
- How can history be perceived from multiple perspectives?
- What are the values of studying history?

IV. Planning

After reading the book *Anne Frank: The Diary of a Young Girl* and studying the Holocaust, provide your students with the following as a writing assignment for creating a position/opinion paper.

Setting: Your school district recently sent letters to parents explaining it will now include a new Holocaust unit as part of the social studies curriculum. Several days after the letters went out, surprised school officials received a number of phoned responses to the announcement. Some parents expressed satisfaction and appreciation, others anger and annoyance. One irate parent shouted that students should not waste time dwelling on misery and studying about horrors that occurred long ago. Yet another caller complimented the school district for exploring so sensitive an issue, adding that awareness might prevent future atrocities. (*Teaching About the Holocaust and Genocide: Introduction.* The Human Rights Series, Vol. I, 1985)

Position/Opinion Paper: The editor of your school newspaper has agreed to publish the selected student responses to the issue. You decide to write a letter to the editor of the school newspaper expressing your opinion. Your letter takes a position either for or against the inclusion of a Holocaust curriculum at your school. In writing your letter, offer substantial personal reasons, as well as reasons taken from your studies of the Holocaust and reading of *Anne Frank: The Diary of a Young Girl.*

(continued on page 84)

V. Playing

- Divide the class into two teams.
- Designate one team as those in favor of teaching the Holocaust and the other team as those against the inclusion of the Holocaust in the social studies curriculum.
- Inform the students that the superintendent of public schools will be holding a meeting with the two teams to discuss the issue. The teacher will play in-role as the superintendent.
- Provide time for the two teams to discuss their viewpoints. Remind them that they are role playing a person having the opinion they have been assigned, and that it may not reflect their own personal opinion. This challenge provides students with the opportunity to view an issue from multiple perspectives.

VI. Evaluation and Follow-Up

- Involve students in a large-group discussion.
- Ask such questions as: "Why do people view history differently?" "How does story help communicate history as opposed to a list of facts?" and "What current events might be possible in historical studies for the future?"
- Invite students to read their letters to the editor as closure to the session.

Social Studies Lesson 4

The Witch of Blackbird Pond (Speare, 1958). The witch hunts of 1692 in Salem, Massachusetts, began when a doctor stated that the hysterical behavior of several teenage girls was due to the "evil eye." Speare captures the fear and persecution of this time in our world.

Instructional Session

I. Topic: Human perspective through story

II. Issues of Exploration

- Character perspectives and interpretaton
- Witch trials of the late 1600s
- Acting to study character

III. Focusing Questions
- How do beliefs govern aspects of one's social life?
- What risks should one take to be who they are?
- What does discrimination mean?

IV. Planning: On concluding the reading of *Witch of Blackbird Pond,* use the following questions and list of characters to involve the class in an analysis of the characters in the story.

Questions: What does each of the characters think of Kit, and how do they feel about her? During the trial, why did these people (characters) choose to either defend or persecute Kit?

Characters:	Matthew	Gideon
	Rachel	Rebecca
	Mercy	Prudence
	Judith	Nat
	William	Hannah

V. Playing
- An actor's job becomes more difficult when he or she is faced with playing a character who has beliefs or behaviors opposite to their own. In *The Witch of Blackbird Pond,* a number of characters may appear on the surface to be mean to Kit. However, their meanness is not because they are bad people. Other factors, such as traditions, upbringing, society, and individual personality traits, are all part of the total character.
- Divide your students into the following four drama groups for the purpose of creating improvised scenes.
  Group 1: will act out the scene when Kit is first accused of being a witch
  Group 2: will enact the scene when Kit is placed in the stocks
  Group 3: will develop a scene from the trial when Kit experiences persecution
  Group 4: will re-create the segment of the trial when Prudence reads and writes, and Kit ultimately is found innocent and freed.
- Each student in each of the four groups will choose a role appropriate to the scene they are assigned.

VI. Evaluation and Follow-Up
- Instruct each student to write a short narrative about how the character they portrayed felt at the end of the trial.

(continued on page 86)

- Encourage students to share the written views of their characters.
- Lead a discussion about how the characters they portrayed might respond to some of today's contemporary issues.
- Develop a whole-group discussion about how the students' views are alike/different from those of the characters they portrayed.

Concluding Thoughts

Dramatic interpretation of the human condition is an approach to involve students in seeing the relevance of studying social studies. Often our instructional approach to social studies is grounded in dates and facts rather than in considering human motives and needs. It is as students experience the life of social studies that they better understand the past, the present, and the possible future of their world. Using drama and literature within the social studies curriculum makes the classroom setting a place to think and actively process content. Social studies becomes real when the "what if" is explored through story and dramatic action.

References

Lasky, Kathryn. 1995. *She's Wearing a Dead Bird on Her Head!* New York: Hyperion Books.

Paulsen, Gary. 1989. *The Winter Room.* New York: Dell Publishing.

Task Force of the National Council for the Social Studies. 1994. *Expectations of Excellence: Curriculum Standards for Social Studies.* Washington, DC: National Council for the Social Studies.

7

Devising Curriculum through Drama and Literature—Science

"Learning science is something students do, not something that is done to them."

—*NATIONAL SCIENCE EDUCATION STANDARDS*, 1996

Focus Question   **In what ways can we integrate drama and literature into a cycle of inquiry to study scientific concepts?**

A Close-Up of Drama

Ms. Douglas's students are studying the human body. The primary instructional material is a themed literature text set. The set includes books such as *Frankenstein* (Shelley, 1831); *The Watsons Go to Birmingham—1963* (Curtis, 1995); *Mama, Let's Dance* (Hermes, 1991); *When the Legends Die* (Borland, 1963); *On To Oregon!* (Morrow, 1926); *The Cay* (Taylor, 1969), and *Good Night, Mr. Tom* (Magorian, 1981). Students have self-selected a text, which created a small reading group. Within these groups, scientific inquiry focuses on how the human body adapts to environmental conditions. The groups present their inquiry studies as a dramatization. For example, one group offers a dramatic reenactment of a story scene, while another offers a short scenario centered around the discovery of penicillin, and a third group shares their work as medical researchers working on a cure for influenza.

The group's culminating activity merges scientific inquiry with literature and dramatic action. Students are learning science through inquiry: observing, inferring, and experimenting. Inquiry is central to the study of science. It creates a setting where students describe objects and events, ask questions, construct explanations, test those explanations against current scientific knowledge, and communicate their ideas. Students are supported to identify their assumptions, use critical and logical thinking, and consider alternative explanations. In this way, an understanding of science is generated by combining scientific knowledge with reasoning and thinking skills (National Science Education Standards, 1996).

When we talk about science we usually think of the content of science. This position is viewed frequently as an encyclopedia of discoveries and technological achievements. Yet, this interpretation fails to take into consideration the principle process of science: inquiry. Science is a process. A process where students acquire and refine new information through concrete experiences.

A major goal in science education is to develop people who can think critically about scientific phenomena. Science, that is, the process, enables students to explore their world as they form educated guesses. In today's technological world, facts alone are not sufficient. Learning science solely from a textbook is like trying to learn to ride a bike from an instructional manual. Science is a process that entails the skills of observing, comparing, classifying, measuring, communicating, inferring, predicting, hypothesizing, and defining and controlling variables to interpret data. And it is precisely these same skills that form the backbone of dramatic action as well as literary interpretation.

Science will more likely be learned and retained if presented in a variety of ways and extended over a period of time. Drama, literature, and science together can provide the learner with a way to explore, experiment, and interpret the science in our day-to-day lives.

Scientific literacy is essential to our everyday living both at home and at the workplace. This information is the knowledge we use to make wise choices and solve problems about the world. An understanding of science and the processes of science opens the door to learn, reason, and think creatively to unravel the questions of today's technological environment. This scientific literacy is critical as we make choices regarding issues such as sun exposure, nuclear materials disposal, water quality, and animal habitats. These decision-making dilemmas place us in a genuine position to apply scientific principles when making personal and social choices.

Learning science involves interaction among the learner, the environment, and the content (Beane, 1992). This blend enables learners to contextualize experience into a system of comprehension. Dramatic literacy is a springboard to an interactive science instructional curriculum. It is this creating of scientific demonstrations, using drama with literature, that nudges our students toward active science learning built on both physical activity as well as mental activity. These hands-on and minds-on lessons provide a context in which students gain new knowledge that they then connect with information they already know.

Drama underscores the relationship between thinking and the social organization of instruction. This student-in-social activity (Minick, 1985) places the learner with others as they create social contexts—zones of proximal development (Vygotsky, 1978) where instruction supports evolving inquiry. Vygotsky's emphasis on the social context of thinking has important methodological significance in designing curriculum to develop new forms of thinking. Drama serves as a channel to weave together scientific inquiry with an instructional context in which a unique form of cooperation develops between student and teacher. This social cooperative approach provides a structure where learners become the objects of pedagogy (Moll, 1990), as they think together and act out the learning of science.

Drama built on children's literature creates a laboratory (Riviere, 1984) where drama becomes the instructional framework to interpret and scrutinize the domains of science and subsequently, their relationship to thinking.

Scientific study is popularly divided into three domains: physical science, life science, and earth and space science. Scientific subject matter focuses on facts, concepts, principles, theories, and models that are important for all students to know, understand, and use. Each of these domains emphasizes the learners' ability to integrate scientific inquiry with scientific content. This scientific literacy is best developed through a cycle of inquiry.

Physical Science with Drama and Literature

Physical science is the study of energy. Fundamental to these studies is the chemistry of compounds, an understanding of energy and its sources, and the uses of electricity.

Chemical reaction is a process in which a new substance is formed. Examples include the rusting of metal, the burning of petroleum, or the decomposing of a dead tree. These reactions give off or absorb energy.

Energy is the generation of action. It exists in many forms such as light, heat, chemical, mechanical, or electrical. When you turn on a lamp, bake a cake, or run a marathon, energy is created and converted into an outcome of a different type.

Electricity is one type of energy. A motor converts electric energy into motion. Other examples include a microphone, telephone, compact disc player, videotape recorder, or computer. These transformations of electric energy into light and sound help people communicate.

The science teacher, using drama as a way to delve into a study of physical science, can use a literary structure to integrate the inquiry method with an analysis of the human condition. *Lyddie* (Paterson, 1991) is the story of an impoverished midnineteenth-century farm girl who overcomes economic and social obstacles. This piece of historical fiction offers a genuine opportunity to investigate the issues of science. The setting of the story deals with technology, physical conditions and health, and societal changes in response to scientific advancements.

Physical Science Lesson

Lyddie (Paterson, 1991) provides students with the opportunity to consider science as a record of the interactive relationship among technological advances, uses of energy, and how humans accommodate this change. Using "Then and Now" dramatic scenarios to depict scenes of technological advancements brings together literature, drama, and science to conduct research.

Instructional Session

  I. Topic: Technology creates changes in society

 II. Issues of Exploration

   • Energy uses
   • Technology and people
   • Science as history
   • Character development

III. Focusing Questions

   • How did the technology of 1843 affect the living and working conditions of people?
   • How have technology advancements since 1843 influenced how we live?

IV. Planning

   • Ask students to find and list the uses of technology in *Lyddie*. Encourage students to remember that what may seem simplistic technology may have been revolutionary in 1843.
   • Use the student-generated lists for students to choose two uses of technology to research that determined the changes between 1843 and the present.

 V. Playing

   • Divide students into groups of five.
   • Within the small groups, present two uses of technology to each student. The group selects two from the ten choices to prepare

two "Then and Now" scenes. One scene depicts the use of technology in 1843, while the other shows the same technology and how it is used today.

- Provide a time for each group to present their "Then and Now" scenarios.

VI. Evaluation and Follow-Up

- Use the "Then" scenes as the focus for student discussions about the effects of technology on the characters in *Lyddie*.
- Examine the "Now" scenes as a resource to compare and contrast our current technology with that of 1843.
- Provide a writing follow-up where students create a story that re-creates a day in their life today as if they were living in 1843.

Life Science with Drama and Literature

Life science involves the study of cells, reproduction, heredity, and living organisms as they live and adapt to their environment. All living things fit within a category that is called a kingdom.

These kingdoms are the animal kingdom, plant kingdom (trees and flowers), fungi kingdom (molds and mildews), protista kingdom (protozoans and most algae), and monera kingdom (bacteria and blue-green algae). The different species, within each of these kingdoms, reproduce their own kind. Reproduction enables a species to carry on. Each kingdom coexists in our world as they cooperate and compete in an ecosystem. Species of both the plant and animal kingdoms adapt to their ecosystems as they continue to live and eventually, evolve.

Using the genre of poetry, *Desert Voices* (Baylor and Parnall, 1981) portrays the shy and quiet creatures of a desert land. This text provides a life science lesson to illustrate how to integrate literature and drama as a vehicle to study a desert ecosystem. This collection of poems would be part of a text set—a collection of literature that presents multiple perspectives on a theme. Students are able to view the theme from different vantage points, consequently increasing their understanding. A desert ecosystem text set may include: *Alejandro's Gift* (Albert, 1994), *Cactus Hotel* (Guiberson, 1991), *The Three Little Javelinas* (Lowell, 1992), and *Downriver* (Hobbs, 1991).

Life Science Lesson

Desert Voices (Baylor and Parnall, 1981) enables students to study an ecosystem from the dramatic point of view of a creature who inhabits such an environment. This type of role playing provides a rich hands-on science exploration of life through the art form of acting.

Instructional Session

I. Topic: Investigate the connection between an animal and its environment

II. Issues of Exploration

- Research on desert animals and their environment
- Vocal interpretation
- Costume and scenic design
- First-person voice

III. Focusing Questions

- Does the type of environment/ecosystem impact the character traits of an animal?
- How do theater artists create animal characters for the stage?

IV. Planning

- Students on an individual basis review *Desert Voices.*
- Students work in whole group to create a round-robin read aloud, where an individual student reads, trying to sound like the animal character. This uses multiple readers per desert animal poem. Each student reads a stanza and passes to the next student, continuing until the book is completed.
- Students then select their favorite desert animal.
- Each student initiates independent research on their desert animal. The research process would include a focus on specific physical traits of the animal and its habitat within the ecosystem.
- Students complete desert animal research and sketch or paint a costume rendering and habitat backdrop. These sketches would serve as potential design models for a play involving the desert ecosystem.

V. Playing

- Students report their research findings using their sketches as visual aids.

- Research reporting culminates with each student reading his or her selected desert animal poem with vocal interpretation.

VI. Evaluation and Follow-Up

- Students are guided to discuss the relationship between desert animals and their habitat. This discussion would include topics such as movement, food and water sources, survival strategies, and shelter.
- Another discussion might focus on how theater artists represent characters and their environment on the stage.
- In small groups students prepare a new edition of *Desert Voices,* using their sketches and writing original first-person verses.

Earth and Space Science with Drama and Literature

The domain of earth and space science includes topics such as space exploration, stars, weather patterns, and changes in the earth. The structure of the earth, its history, and role in the solar system are crucial to a scientific study of the world as we know it.

The earth is forever changing as a result of physical and chemical weathering, erosion, and deposition. These changes create features on the surface such as canyons, mountains, and flatlands. Changes below the surface, such as underground springs, caves, and molten rocks are created as well. Additionally, large sections of the earth's surface move continuously and eventually may cause rock slides, earthquakes, or volcanoes. Human impacts on the earth also are relevant to a study of earth and space science.

Humans change the earth through the building of dams to supply water and electricity to people. At times, these changes may be beneficial, but other uses of the earth may result in water and air pollution that is harmful to our planet and its people.

Meteorologists collect weather data at both the earth's surface and above to forecast changes that may affect us. Astronomers explore space from the ground by using different kinds of telescopes, as well as satellites, to study the stars and planets in our solar system. By studying and traveling into space, our knowledge of earth cycles such as the sun's rotation, the varying seasons, and weather phenomenons is greatly enhanced.

Using literature and drama as a method to breach the topic of pollution and its harm to our earth prevents the topic from becoming too academic. A story mixed with improvisation and writing makes this earth science study more personal and accessible for the learner.

Earth and Space Science Lesson

Just A Dream (Van Allsburg, 1990) is the story of Walter, a young protagonist who is not concerned about the environment. He is a litterbug. However, one night Walter wishes he could see the future, and his wish comes true. However, the future is not quite what he had imagined.

Instructional Session

I. Topic: Man and his Environment

II. Issues of Exploration

- Environmental awareness
- Natural resources usage
- Interaction between humans and their environment
- Critical thinking
- Drama as learning demonstration

III. Focusing Question: What will our world be like if we fail to recognize our impact on the natural environment?

IV. Planning

- Ask students to push desks to the sides of the room in order to create a large open space that can be used as a playing area.
- Instruct the group of students to find their own personal playing space.
- Teacher says, "We are going to imagine ourselves in different environments using our senses to feel them. We will begin our environmental travels using visual imagery followed by physically interacting with the environment. First, you need to seat yourself on the floor in your own space, close your eyes and imagine yourself in the environment as I describe it. Now when I say go, you will open your eyes, stand, and begin to move through the imagined environment."
- Provided are some environmental descriptions that can be used in this visual imagery warm-up activity.
- Environment description ideas:

  A Trash Dump "You are in the midst of a gigantic, open dumping area. There are old tires, broken furniture, piles of smelly, rotten food, and mountains of full plastic garbage bags."

  A Smokestack Forest "You are now surrounded by hundreds of smokestacks that are belching forth thick, cloudy, gray haze.

The smell of the haze is foul and your eyes begin to burn and itch."

A Freeway "You now find yourself standing in the middle of a huge traffic jam on a five-lane expressway. Cars, trucks, and vans are honking their horns, racing their engines, and moving bumper to bumper."

V. Playing

- Divide the students into seven small groups.
- Provide each group with a copy of *Just A Dream*. Assign one of the first seven double-paged text illustrations that depict environmental dangers to a group. Each group is assigned a different text illustration.
- Have each group develop a living drama of their text illustration. Begin the dramatization frozen, according to the illustration. Encourage students to create additional roles other than those depicted so that all group members have a character to play. Students may also wish to personify inanimate textual objects such as a smokestack, the last tree in the forest, and an automobile.
- Provide a time for each group to present their environmental dramatization.

VI. Evaluation and Follow-Up

- Ask students to write about which environmental danger they feel is most pressing, and what the world may be like if we don't modify our behavior. Encourage students to elaborate on their responses by identifying their reasons for selection as well as a solution for the problem.
- Students first share their writings with others in a small-group setting, and then conduct a large-group discussion that summarizes their thoughts and feelings.

Concluding Thoughts

Students in our classroom need to learn how to think scientifically, reason logically, make observations, gather and organize these observations, conduct experiments and draw conclusions, and make an intelligent guess to determine what those conclusions might be—supported, rejected or left undetermined. Most importantly, students must experience the joy of learning science.

Drama and literature open the door to science instruction where the facts and rules of scientific inquiry come to life. Science curriculum, along with drama and literature, is a process, a way of thinking and acting. It is scientific method, dramatic action, and literary response that makes doing science a pleasure. This actual interpretation of science inspires a natural fascination with learning. The essential element in science instruction is to develop encounters where students engage in the content. Drama and literature promote students' engagement with the field of science. When students' interest is engaged in the topic then the questions—inquiry—are automatic.

References

Albert, Richard E. 1994. *Alejandro's Gift.* San Francisco: Chronicle Books.

Baylor, Byrd, and Peter Parnall. 1981. *Desert Voices.* New York: Aladdin Books.

Borland, Hal. 1963. *When the Legends Die.* New York: Bantam Books.

Curtis, Christopher P. 1995. *The Watsons Go to Birmingham: 1963.* New York: Delacorte Press.

Guiberson, Brenda Z. 1991. *Cactus Hotel.* New York: Henry Holt.

Hermes, Patricia. 1991. *Mama, Let's Dance.* New York: Scholastic.

Hobbs, Will. 1991. *Downriver.* New York: Bantam Books.

Lowell, Susan. 1992. *The Three Little Javelinas.* Flagstaff, AZ: Northland Press.

Magorian, Michelle. 1981. *Good Night, Mr. Tom.* New York: HarperTrophy.

Morrow, Honore. 1926. *On to Oregon.* New York: Beech Tree Books.

National Research Council. 1996. National Science Education Standards. Washington, DC: National Academy Press.

Paterson, Katherine. 1991. *Lyddie.* New York: Penguin Books.

Taylor, Theodore. 1969. *The Cay.* New York: Avon Books.

8
Curriculum and Drama Development—Mathematics

"When mathematics evolves naturally from problem situations that have meaning . . . it becomes relevant and links knowledge to many kinds of situations."
STANDARDS FOR SCHOOL MATHEMATICS, 1989

Focus Question   How can drama, incorporated within literary readings, create natural opportunities to use mathematics in problem-solving applications?

A Close-Up of Drama

Groups of students have developed and administered a survey on adolescent smoking and tabulated the results. The different groups are presenting their findings. One group presents the findings as a panel discussion at a national press conference at the White House. Another group presents their findings as a commercial for television viewing while one other group presents a role playing of smokers and nonsmokers debating their findings at a public hearing.

The learning outcome for this dramatized mathematics lesson has students working with a firsthand situation where math skills are used to collect, organize, and interpret data. The mathematical concepts become a springboard to use drama as a way to communicate data to a larger audience. Literacy also plays a pivotal role in the development of the survey within this instructional sequence, as students work with mathematics as a natural measurement of a real-life dilemma.

This chapter will focus on drama as a tool in mathematics instruction to address problem solving, communication, and reasoning. Instructional episodes will illustrate how to integrate the learning of mathematical concepts with drama. Fusing mathematics with dramatics situates learning in a context in which students engage in constructing knowledge through inquiry, investigation, analysis of situations, and problem solving. Drama presents learners with opportunities to build their knowledge by staging mathematical concepts via group or individual presentations. This concrete curriculum—real experience—helps students talk and write about their thinking while discussing with others what they are doing as they do it.

To combine drama with mathematics instruction is to bring together two natural processes where problems are proposed and solutions offered. When mathematical problems are studied through drama, the results are a complex give-and-take of acting out one's thinking. First, the mathematical concepts will suggest the type of dramatics that may evolve. The mathematical theory operates as a guide, whose real-world function defines the drama and sets in motion the weaving of a dramatized mathematics problem, which is generated through purposeful playing (O'Neill, 1991).

Mathematical concepts, in the classroom, are the reason to use drama, and in turn become the text that will define the nature and limits of the drama. The playing of the mathematical concepts helps to frame the participants in appropriate roles relative to the action, and at the same time opens up certain expectations and possibilities while excluding others.

Drama creates a response to the mathematics. It will share some significant features with the world of the mathematical concepts, but may build on select dimensions while overlooking others. The dramatic world will illuminate the theory and, above all, give students ready access to it (Rogers and O'Neill, 1993).

Students begin with the mathematical concepts and then move to incorporating drama as a strategy to construct an understanding of the ideas. They are able to bring their personal understandings of the mathematical concepts into the drama activities, which supply an opportunity to live through the learning. This living mathematics is similar to Rosenblatt's (1978) transactional literary theory. When students operate as the learning ingredients, they have an immediate and actual experience of the mathematical concept. This contact creates a situation where the theory is accessible to students as they construct, through drama, a bridge to abstract thinking through their own understanding.

Drama enables students to construct mathematical ideas, theories, principles, and conceptual understandings. It generates opportunities where students test their personal understanding of mathematics in a public forum. This adds to the shaping of their thinking as well as their comprehension. It is these dramatic ventures that will empower students to learn mathematics as they work through the theory and then form their own knowledge and insight (Edmiston, 1991).

A learning-teaching environment in the study of mathematics needs to institute collaborative, cooperative, and interactive instruction. This type of learning context contributes to more successful student performance (Miller, 1987). A dramatic mathematics curriculum offers learners multiple opportunities to explain mathematical ideas to others, listen to strategies presented by classmates, ask questions of others, and agree and disagree on solutions to problems.

Literature is a primary source of materials that a teacher can use to design lessons where drama provides the means to play with mathematics. Children's literature becomes the common ground on which to organize an interdisciplinary curriculum where mathematics and drama merge to investigate the topic of study. The literature selection acts as the context where everyday mathematical problems are tested through dramatic actions. Rather than simply determining the calculations for a math problem, a teacher would identify mathematical concepts that fit naturally within the literary text. These are studied through drama. Mathematics and dramatics work as a team to provide students with different ways to think and respond to the concepts.

Problem Solving with Drama and Mathematics

Problem solving is one process in which students are able to apply mathematics to everyday questions and real-life matters. The possibility to participate in a mathematical need-to-know provides a setting where students are able to grasp firsthand the concept under study. This mathematical inquiry motivates students to view mathematics as a practical process with functional outcomes. Thinking strategies such as (1) looking for patterns, (2) hypothesizing an educated guess; (3) making proportional sketches, or (4) creating diagrams and tables contribute to a context of problem solving (Standards for School Mathematics, 1989).

Drama and literature combined provide a natural study vehicle to understanding mathematical concepts. The book *Soda Jerk* (Rylant, 1990) is a collection of twenty-eight poems in which Rylant depicts her teenage years in West Virginia. It captures life in a 1960s drugstore in Appalachia. From behind the counter, the soda jerk's lens opens a stage to speculate on life's inconsistencies. Within the dramatic response to this literature, mathematical processes are studied through application.

Mathematics Lesson 1

Soda Jerk (Rylant, 1990) provides students with the opportunities to respond to how setting—the *where*—is a dynamic influence on our lives. A dramatic, literature, and mathematical connection is generated through these poems as students design a theatrical setting using mathematical skills to render to scale a sketch of the drugstore setting. A teacher prompts students' thinking by asking questions such as (1) How do we interact with our environment?, (2) How does environment play a role in creating mood?, and (3) How can an environment reflect the personality of the characters who inhabit it? Discussion of these questions sets the stage for students to create scenic designs for dramatic playings of the poems.

Instructional Session

I. Topic: Space as story

II. Issues of Exploration

- Proportion
- Scale
- Scenic design and construction
- Interpretation

III. Focusing Questions

- What is the design of Maywell's drugstore?
- How does the drugstore setting encourage the telling of these stories?

IV. Planning

- Ask students to sketch their visual image of what Maywell's drugstore looks like and to include the counter(s), furniture, doors, windows, shelving, and other furnishings.
- Guide students from this abstract image to find a room that is similar in size to their envisioned drugstore. Students measure the dimensions of the room they select, as well as other concrete objects similar to the furnishings in their sketch. These measurements will provide students with data to produce a scaled blueprint (floor plan) of Maywell's drugstore.
- To draw their floor plan, students use a scale where 1 inch equals 1 foot. This scale will fit comfortably on a piece of poster board. Students can display their completed blueprints in the room.

Through discussion, students compare and contrast how their drugstore designs reflect their interpretation of the storyline.

V. Playing

- Divide students into groups of five.
- Presenting their individual blueprints within groups, students select one floor plan to serve as the design to use to physically construct Maywell's drugstore in the classroom. The students will need to improvise furnishings and other elements by using items such as chairs, tables, cardboard boxes, step ladders, and other such equipment.
- Identifying two of Rylant's poem to develop for a dramatic rendering, student groups construct their playing space.
- Provide a time for each group to present their *Soda Jerk* dramatization.

VI. Evaluation and Follow-Up

- Encourage student groups to discuss what would happen to the staging of the poems if one of the other floor plans were used.
- Address, as a large group, how the different scene designs contribute to a different playing of the poetry selections. This discussion allows students to explore how perspective influences interpretation.
- Involve the large group in composing a poem on the topic of setting—a special place. Students, from this demonstration, author collaborative verses.
- Providing the materials for students, these student-authored verses become the materials for students to create new floor plans and scenic renderings. If students are motivated, they may then construct these settings. A playing of student-composed poetry would serve as follow-up.

Communication with Drama and Mathematics

Communication, within mathematics, provides a means to weave literacy— listening, speaking, reading, and writing—into the curriculum as tools to work with concepts and express understandings. Students writing mathematics are able to demonstrate their thinking and in turn, clarify their thinking as they write their ideas. To promote teaching mathematical communications, a teacher simply asks questions or poses problem situations where students discuss the *how* and *why*. These deliberations spill over into students' writing problems and showing how they could be solved.

Students working in collaborative group activities are able to think mathematically through listening, talking, reading, and writing. This curricular design places the spotlight on student presentations where they rehearse their thinking, portray their knowledge, and communicate mathematically.

To further illustrate the process of integrating drama within the mathematics curriculum, our second lesson sampler builds on Natalie Babbitt's *The Eyes of the Amaryllis* (1977). This novel is a ghost story with real-life events that can't be explained. This provocative tale involves students in generating hypotheses that lead to possible solutions.

Mathematics Lesson 2

The Eyes of the Amaryllis (Babbitt, 1977) is the story of a young female protagonist who spends time at her grandmother's home located on the New England coast. The Thanksgiving holiday provides a setting for Jenny to delve into a hidden family secret—the death of her grandfather, who drowned while at sea on his ship, the *Amaryllis*. This fantasy provides a natural context for a mathematics teacher to develop instructional materials, which naturally enables students to play with the "if . . . then" statements of the text. This activity leads to a plausible hypothesis that suggests a conclusion. For example, in *The Eyes of the Amaryllis,* Jenny's grandmother is waiting for her drowned husband to give her a sign that he is still with her in spirit. One day on the beach, Grandmother finds an amaryllis blossom. She believes this is her sign. If Jenny's grandfather is with his wife in spirit, then he will send her a sign—an "if . . . then" statement.

Instructional Session

I. Topic: Addressing mathematical concepts of hypothesis by generating evidence and conclusion making with "if . . . then" statements.

II. Issues of Exploration

- Create plot summaries through tableau
- Create "if . . . then" statements
- Distinguish evidence within storyline
- Live demonstration of hypothesis and conclusion

III. Focusing Questions

- How do we draw conclusions from what we see, hear, or read?
- Does a hypothesis always lead to a proven conclusion?

IV. Planning

- While reading the text, each student will select five story events that are primary to the ending. From these they write "if . . . then" statements.
- In small groups students read their "if . . . then" statements to select the five that capture best the tone of *The Eyes of the Amaryllis*.

V. Playing

- Using the five "if . . . then" statements, small groups develop tableaux (frozen pictures) of the different statements.
- Presenting each tableau, one group member reads the accompanying "if . . . then" statement.
- Each tableau is acted out for one minute, with the story developing as a series of frozen pictures and improvisations.

VI. Evaluation and Follow-Up

- Students openly compare and contrast the varying "if . . . then" statements of the tableaux.
- Extending the mathematical concepts, the small groups now rewrite the five "if . . . then" statements as "converse" statements, which would then be enacted as new statements. A converse statement takes the *if* part of the statement and moves it to the *then* section and vice versa. Allow for follow-up discussion after the reenactments in which students and teacher address whether the hypothesis remains a true statement or what new meaning is created.

Reasoning with Drama and Mathematics

Reasoning is the keystone to knowing and doing mathematics. Students need opportunities to experience informed guessing as an open-ended approach to mathematical curriculum. Students learn to make predictions and illustrate initial interpretations, based on logic, as they practice the principles of problem solving. Students need numerous types of learning experiences to refine their ability to analyze problem situations, suggest potential solutions, and consider others' ideas. This cycle of deductive and inductive reasoning is intertwined with students' literacy development.

Reasoning is a fundamental skill that we use throughout our lives. This core competency focuses on identifying the central factors—what is happening in a situation and how to consider and address the circumstances. Drama

---

Mathematics Lesson 3

The Giver (Lowry, 1993) uses the mathematical strategy of reasoning to look at multiple possibilities for considering and solving a dilemma.

Instructional Session

I. Topic: Making informed choices through reasoning

II. Issues of Exploration

- Develop reasoned thinking skills
- Make informed decisions
- Present a dramatic debate

III. Focusing Questions

- Why should we look at both sides of a coin before reaching a conclusion?
- What makes a good debate?

IV. Planning

- Discuss as a large group the decisions Jonas makes in the course of the book.
- List at least five major decisions that the character makes. A major character decision is defined as one that has multiple choices, and each choice will make a significant difference in the life of the character. List for each decision another possible choice Jonas could have made besides the one in the story.
- Divide the class into two teams. For each major decision, one half of the class creates arguments for the choice Jonas made in the actual book, while the other half develops arguments for the alternate choice Jonas could have made.

V. Playing

- Using the two sets of arguments developed by each team, conduct a formal debate about each of the major decisions Jonas

---

makes. To create a formal debating atmosphere use the following guidelines:

1. The teacher serves as moderator.
2. For each major decision, one team starts and has two minutes to discuss their opinions. Then the other team has one minute to respond (rebuttal).
3. The team who responded (rebutted) then starts a two-minute discussion of the next major decision with the one-minute response (rebuttal) by the other team. This alternating technique continues until all the major decisions are debated.
4. At the conclusion of the debate each team gets two minutes to share any concluding comments.

VI. Evaluation and Follow-Up

- Discuss how reasoning affects decision making.
- Discuss the analytical thinking skills used to develop a convincing argument.
- Extend the exploration of reasoning by encouraging the students to write an alternate ending to *The Giver*. This may perhaps incorporate the varying opinions presented during the debate.

and literature open doors for students to develop this thinking proficiency, which is a natural facet of mathematics.

Another dramatic mathematics session is one that uses debate as the fundamental way to hone reasoning skills.

Concluding Thoughts

Math, drama, and literature together can create a dynamic mathematics learning environment. Problem solving, communication, and reasoning form the core of mathematics. And it is these same skills that are fundamental to envisioning a piece of literature or interpreting a dramatic scenario. The teaching of mathematics can be constructed with real-life experience through drama and literature. This focus evokes personal meaning for both critical thinking as well as creative. Our daily lives are filled with situations where thinking— problem solving, communication, and reasoning—forms the crux of all decisions from a personal level to a national level and on to the international level. To develop students who are thinkers able to acquire and use knowledge means educating minds rather than training memories. Being good at thinking calls for generating numerous explanations and demonstrating an intellectual curiosity resulting in scholarly inquiry. It is when we combine the elements of drama and literature that a study of mathematical concepts leads to quality thinking. By teaching with an emphasis on problem solving through drama and literature, students learn to recognize when they may need to use different mathematical concepts or procedures that result in a strong conceptual basis for reconstructing their knowledge at a later time.

References

Babbitt, Natalie. 1977. *The Eyes of the Amaryllis*. New York: Scholastic.

Edminston, Brian. 1991. "What Have You Travelled? A Teacher-Researcher Study of Structuring Drama for Reflection and Learning." Unpublished doctoral dissertation. Ohio State University.

Karp, Karen, et al. 1998. *Feisty Females: Inspiring Girls to Think Mathematically*. Portsmouth, NH: Heinemann.

Lowry, Lois. 1993. *The Giver*. Boston: Houghton Mifflin.

Miller, J. 1987. "Women as Teachers/Researchers: Gaining a Sense of Ourselves." *Teacher Education Quarterly* 14 (2): 52–58.

O'Neill, Cecily. 1991. "Structure and Spontaneity: Improvisation in Theatre and Education." Unpublished dissertation, Exeter University.

Rogers, T., and C. O'Neill. 1993. Creating Multiple Worlds. In G. E. Newell, and R. K. Durst (Eds.), *Exploring Texts: The Role of Discussion and Writing in the Teaching and Learning of Literature*. Norwood, MA: Christopher-Gordon Publishers, Inc.

Rosenblatt, Louise. 1978. *The Reader, the Text, the Poem*. Carbondale, IL: Southern Illinois University Press.

Rylant, Cynthia. 1990. *Soda Jerk*. New York: Beech Tree Books.

Working Groups of the Commission on Standards for School Mathematics of the National Council of Teachers of Mathematics. 1989. *Curriculum and Evaluation: Standards for School Mathematics*. Reston, VA: The National Council of Teachers of Mathematics.

9

Second Language Learning in Action

"Language and communication are at the heart of the human experience."

STATEMENT OF PHILOSOPHY
STANDARDS FOR FOREIGN LANGUAGE LEARNING, 1993

Focus Question How can drama and literature assist students who will become more linguistically and culturally equipped to communicate successfully in our global world?

A Close-Up of Drama

Ms. Sanchez's Spanish class students read *The Three Little Javelinas* (Lowell, 1992). Students use the text to create a narrative pantomime activity, in which some students will read the book aloud while other students act out the story using physical action. Small groups of students study the Spanish language to translate key words, written in English, into Spanish. When the story is read aloud during the narrative pantomime playing, Spanish is the language of use.

The students' performance of *The Three Little Javelinas* reflects a production where students use their study of Spanish while working in groups. This action provides for students to connect with other disciplines while acquiring information to develop insight into the nature of language and culture. Drama and literature in the foreign language classroom brings students into a learning environment where they are engaging in conversations—working with language and culture . This instructional approach incorporates the Five Cs of Second Language Education: communication, cultures, connections, comparisons, and communities.

The linguistic and social knowledge necessary for meaningful human-to-human communication builds on "knowing how, when, and what to say to whom" (Standards for Foreign Language Learning, 1993). Traditionally, second language instruction was built on a study of grammar and vocabulary. Today, the Coalition of Foreign Language Organizations (1993) encourages a more hands-on approach where the learning of a second language is the ability to communicate in meaningful and appropriate ways with users of other languages. The prevailing principle to guide foreign language curriculum development is communication, where the why, the who, and the when form the content for designing purposeful instructional episodes.

Students study a foreign language for several reasons. Yet, fundamental to students' particular motivations, studies in a second language will be more substantial when the curriculum revolves around communication, cultures, connections, comparisons, and communities. An individual desiring to become multilingual will need to comprehend the whole of the language—the customs, traditions, behaviors, and ways of being within the particular culture of the foreign language being studied.

The art of communication is pivotal to second-language study, whether this communication occurs face-to-face, in writing, or through reading the literature. To learn a language, one naturally absorbs fluency through the use of the language. It is difficult, if not impossible, to learn a second language without progressing through the intuitive stages of language acquisition. The learning of phrases establishes a knowledge base where more extensive use will result.

During the study of another language, it is essential that students gain a knowledge and understanding of the cultures that use the language. One cannot master a language without also developing an understanding and appreciation of the cultural context in which the language occurs. To study a language without studying the culture attributes is like learning to play a piano without a piano. A language is culture specific, where the language represents and captures the culture of its users.

The study of a second language builds connections to bodies of knowledge that may be unavailable to the monolingual English speaker. Great pieces of literature as well as exemplary thinkers may remain unknown. The study of a second language becomes a path to expanding and deepening students' understanding of, and exposure to, other areas of knowledge. Knowledge of a second language offers a window of opportunity to the world and broadens their access to information.

Another cornerstone of a second language curriculum is the ability to view the world through multiple ways. It is through acts of comparing and contrasting the language being studied that students develop insights into the nature of the language and concept of culture. Studying a second language expands their knowledge of cultures as they discover perspectives, practices, and products similar and different from their own.

Drama-literature offers a unique approach to teach a second language. Drama-literature lessons establish a context for community where it becomes the fabric of interpersonal communication. Community is a phenomenon of the spirit which must be deliberately sought. And it is through drama and literature that students will learn how to transform themselves into a community recognizing the importance of knowing how to live in a global world. These connections create life and growth.

The curriculum to study a second language, as advocated by the American Council on the Teaching of Foreign Languages (1993), is an integrative approach where skills and fluency are embedded within cultural immersion. The use of drama and literature offers purposeful engagements with learning a second language within a cultural context. They bring the studies of a second language alive through genuine involvement to foster a comprehensive experience. These vehicles of learning convey knowledge in an active mode, where a study of language involves an understanding of a group of people and their history. Additionally, drama and literature instruction makes an enriching and enlivening avenue to gaining essential understanding about ourselves and the world.

Drama-literature lessons allow students to situate themselves in the being of a second language, where a broad perspective of understanding will be achieved and connections between concepts and new information becomes apparent. When a study of a second language is interwoven with drama and literature, the study becomes more than just that of content. It becomes the language—the culture—and leads to more in-depth intercultural understanding. The drama-literature lessons become a mode of learning. It is through students' active identification with imagined roles and situation in a study of a second language that they will learn to explore issues, events, and relationships well beyond the grammar and speaking of a second language. These lessons involve students in a use of their knowledge and experience of the world in order to create a world where another language is spoken.

Drama-literature is essentially social and leads to communication and negotiation of meaning. A defining feature of drama-literature, as an instructional mode, is the kind of learning it encourages. These include inquiry, critical and constructive thought, problem solving, skills of comparison, interpretation, judgment and discrimination, and extended learning and research (O'Neill and Lambert, 1982). The experience nurtures understanding human behavior by becoming a part of the unknown. This understanding involves natural changes in traditional ways of thinking and feeling, leading to a greater understanding of self and other. Drama-literature is a constructive means to make connections between second language instruction and students. Learning a second language becomes more likely to happen when students are participating in an interpretative process of the language. Drama-literature instruction motivates learners to create a learning context where they are asked to think, talk, manipulate concrete materials, and share viewpoints in order to make a decision (Siks, 1983).

Drama-literature's unique draw is its potential to place learners in multiple contexts—in situations that generate forms of thought, feeling, and language beyond those usually generated in a traditional second language instructional setting. Students are able to try on the language, the cultural experiences, while studying factual knowledge and concepts (Smith & Herring, 1993). Drama-literature examines human issues and behaviors in specific social contexts. They offer an ideal setting to study a second language where students are able to make discoveries about the language being studied.

Communication: Second Language Studies and Drama-Literature

This instructional strand engages students in conversations in which they are able to express feelings and emotions as well as provide information and exchange ideas. Studies in a second language need to create places where students are able to experiment with speaking and listening—interpreting the spoken word on a variety of topics. It is the opportunity to use a language in actual scenarios that enables students to become fluent in a second language.

Second Language Lesson 1

Gary Soto's *Local News* (1993) is a collection of stories that capture the nuances in the everyday lives of boys and girls growing up in a Mexican-American neighborhood. This perceptive and sensitive chronicle of ordinary life offers a natural starting point to study Mexican Spanish where the focus is on communication—discussions regarding sibling rivalry, self-image, growing up, and different cultures.

Instructional Session

   I. Topic: Communication in languages other than English

   II. Issues of Exploration

   • Writing a second language
   • Speaking a second language

III. Focusing Question

- How can students present information and ideas as well as express feelings and emotions to an audience using a second language?

IV. Planning

- After reading *Local News,* ask students to select their favorite story from the collection.
- Have students write either a newspaper article or a newscast story in the language under study. The article or newscast should be a summary of the original story and take approximately two minutes to read silently or speak aloud.

V. Playing

Option 1 (for newspaper article)

- Students publish an in-class newspaper or newsletter containing their summary articles of *Local News.*
- Each student reads their article aloud to the class on the day the publication is completed.

Option 2 (for newscast)

- Divide students into teams with four or five members.
- Each team creates a newscast program with each team member presenting a report on their particular story. Suggest that each report perhaps be presented using a different method of reporting (e.g., as a news anchor, an on-the-street reporter, an interviewer, etc.).
- Videotape these newscast programs for later viewing.

VI. Evaluation and Follow-Up

- Compare and contrast the written and spoken elements of using Spanish or the language under study.
- Allow students to discuss what forms of communication they are most fond of or having trouble understanding.
- Using the newscast option, provide students with the opportunity to view a video recording of a news program spoken in English, and have teams of students re-create the program in the language under study.

Culture: Second Language Studies and Drama-Literature

One cannot be fluent in a second language without also studying the culture of the language. It is the relationships between practices and perspectives of culture and the use of a language that is the study of a second language. The cultural practices are derived from traditional ideas and attitudes of a culture. The cultural practices include patterns of behavior that form the ways to be within a culture. It is the varying aspects of culture—the use of discourse, the social pecking order, rites of passage, and use of space—that represent the language (knowledge) of what to do when and where.

The products of a culture studied reveal the culture. These products may be both tangible or intangible. They may include paintings, pieces of literature, a traditional dance, a sacred ritual, or a system of education to present a few cultural products. It is the presence of the product within the culture that portrays the underlying beliefs and perspectives of a culture and its practices. Study of a second language involves students in using the language as they also learn basic attitudes toward the larger world around them. How will they consider the peoples of the world and events within it?

Second Language Lesson 2

I Used to Be a Superwoman (Velasquez, 1997) is a collection of poems that reads like diary entries in the life of a Chicana. The poet allows us to travel with her as she traverses the phases of her life. In each poem, the feelings and the reader speak to each other.

Instructional Session

I. Topic: Gain knowledge and understanding of other cultures

II. Issues of Exploration

- Oral interpretation
- Perspectives of a culture
- Practices of a culture
- Products of a culture

III. Focusing Question

- How can students demonstrate an understanding of a culture through the written and spoken language of the culture being studied?

IV. Planning

- Divide students into pairs and have them select two poems from *I Used to Be a Superwoman* that depict or describe a practice, product, or perspective of the Chicano culture.
- Instruct the pairs to rehearse a reading of the poems in which one individual reads the Mexican-Spanish version of the poem while the other reads the English version. The two readers take turns reading each stanza. For the first poem, one reader speaks all the Mexican-Spanish while the other reader speaks the English.
- Students reverse reader roles for the reading of the second poem.

V. Playing: Pairs of students share their interpretive readings aloud with the rest of the class.

VI. Evaluation and Follow-Up

- Discuss what aspects of the Chicano culture are demonstrated through the interpretive readings.
- What emotional qualities are evident in the written and spoken Chicano poetry?
- Have students try their hand at writing a poem that depicts a practice, product, or perspective of their own personal culture. Have them write the poem in their native language as well as the language under study.

Connections: Second Language and Drama-Literature

Learning is an integrative process where all disciplines form the spokes of the wheel. Studying a second language cannot be approached in a void. Rather, these studies need to connect to other subject areas where students are able to build upon the knowledge being studied across the curriculum. A key issue is an interdisciplinary process that encourages students to make use of a second language study to acquire knowledge stemming from the other disciplines of the curriculum.

The art of being able to recognize several distinctive viewpoints is a critical outcome of second language studies. These windows of understanding enable students to recognize the similarities of all cultures and lead to a world where differences are valued. When second language studies are approached through a drama-literature curriculum, the kinds of learning that may arise will not derive primarily from teacher-directed instruction. Rather, students are ready through enactments to become proficient users of a second language, seek out materials of interest, analyze multiple perspectives, and compare accessible information in their own language while assessing linguistic and cultural differences.

Drama-literature as an instructional format suggests an artistic approach to education by presenting alternative modes of expressing experience and providing balance to the total curriculum. The use of drama-literature as a form of inquiry learning and presentation format reveals the contrariness of the human condition and illuminates edifices and dichotomies of social, political, and cultural structures in a safe setting (Eisner, 1979).

Second Language Lesson 3

Sisters (Paulsen, 1993) is told in both English and Spanish. The story of two young protagonists exposes the similarities of lives whether on the street or in a high school gymnasium. This story of similarities and contrasts reveals that we are more alike than different, illuminating the connections of life among all people.

Instructional Session

I. Topic: Connect with other disciplines and acquire information

II. Issues of Exploration

- Recognize distinctive viewpoints
- Role playing
- Gain knowledge about cultures through language

III. Focusing Question: How can the study of language increase knowledge and help make connections between cultures?

IV. Planning

- After reading *Sisters,* discuss the connections found between the two characters while on the surface these two characters seem so different.
- Assign each student the task of creating a character profile of someone with fifty percent of their own personal qualities and fifty percent fictional qualities.
- Pair students together for the purpose of conducting interviews of one another's newly created characters.

V. Playing

- Each pair will take turns interviewing one another for five minutes in the language being studied.

- When the interviewing process is complete, each individual will write an introduction for their partner.
- Pairs will take turns introducing each other to the rest of the class speaking in the language they are studying.

VI. Evaluation and Follow-Up

- Provide the pairs with an opportunity to discuss the similarities and differences found among their characters. What perhaps are the reasons for either the similarities or the differences or both?
- Encourage students to interview someone from another culture outside the classroom environment.

Comparisons: Second Language and Drama-Literature

Drama-literature presents an opportunity to generate a comparative examination of languages through both an introspective, personal as well as public discourse that equates the multilayered practices of culture. By using dramatic interpretation of literature, instruction systematically helps students gain an understanding of how languages work. The use of drama-literature heightens an awareness of the varying social, political, and cultural tensions present in language. They provide the learners with language, rhythm, and movement to study and to question *what is,* as well as *what might be.* The process of studying a second language begins with learning experiences built around personal involvement to enhance acquisition and retention of new facts and information regarding the language.

Second language students need abundant chances to research and to understand words. Being able to use the language will come as they struggle with comparative interpretations of words, actions, and practices associated with the language. A second language learner's first act of understanding a language is to relate symbolically to something or someone outside of herself. This will appear first as language in a drama-literature playing. The playing becomes a way to understand and use the language while developing an understanding of the never-ending struggle to bring together both languages.

A learning environment conducive to constructing the how, what, and when of learning a second language offers students opportunities to discover what language appears to be by participating in worthwhile experiences that exist via drama-literature playings. Second language instruction needs to tap a student's feelings through identification with things and people. Drama-literature curriculum provides students with quality materials grounded in human experiences, while promoting a capacity to cope with understanding how to use and understand the language studied. It is through identification with quality language learning experiences that a student is able to go beyond what is expected and to respond in a dramatic-literature format to develop the processes of thinking, feeling, and experiencing the second language.

This process approach to studying another language leads to extending and enriching language studies through dramatic-literature play activities. Learning a language happens as we share and reflect on our attempts to use and understand the language. This reflective process encourages an integrative process where students are supported in thinking critically about how languages work as a unique dimension of culture.

Second Language Lesson 4

Rising Voices (Hirschfelder and Singer, 1992) is a collection of writings by young Native Americans that convey a range of feelings, from pride in the old ways to conflict with the present. The words of these young people speak about how it feels to be an Indian trying to be in harmony with both worlds. Their words express anger, regret, and hope while offering insight into a race of people whose opinions, until recently, have too often been overlooked. This collection portrays the struggle for personal identity that is known to all races. It is this comparative view, capturing the similarities and differences in perspectives, practices, and products that ignites a study of language and culture.

Instructional Session

I. Topic: Develop insight into the nature of language and culture through comparisons

II. Issues of Exploration

- Comparisons of a second language and one's own
- Comparisons of a culture studied and one's own
- Cultural writing

III. Focusing Question: What can one understand about a culture and its language by comparing it with their own culture and language?

IV. Planning

- Divide class into small groups for the purposes of acting out passages from *Rising Voices*. The book is written in sections— Identity, Family, Homelands, Ritual and Ceremony, Education, and Harsh Realities.

- Instruct each group to select one passage from each section and develop a dramatic scene that tells the cultural story of the selected passage.

V. Playing

- Each small group shares with the rest of the class its dramatic scenes of *Rising Voices.*
- Share all scenes for each section of the book before moving onto the next section.

VI. Evaluation and Follow-Up

- Instruct each student to write a poem or short narrative for each of the section headings in *Rising Voices.* These writings should be based on their own personal experiences.
- Either act out or read these new cultural writings as a whole-class project/event.
- Compare the varying cultural viewpoints illustrated through the students' writings and those in the literature text.

Communities: Second Language and Drama-Literature

The last strand for second language learning is the use of studies to be used by students both within and beyond the school setting. Language is a process where the goal is communication. And in the study of languages an intended outcome is the ability to use a language as a tool for communication with speakers of the language. It is through the speaking of a language that a community of understanding and acceptance will evolve. When we join a language community we are able to deepen our understanding of human interaction and the meaning of life. The ability and skill to participate in social interaction where the sharing and negotiating of meaning occurs helps us to see the world in a new way, as members of a different language community.

Drama-literature instructional strategies encourage a native approach to search for and identify with insights of world cultures. They provide an infinite variety of openings to learn of events, issues, and relationships that are the structure of a particular language community. Community is fundamental to building a lifelong interest in studying and using a second language to provide for personal enrichment as well as being able to communicate with others. Second language studies that offer students a variety of communication systems facilitate an approach to learning where the imagination enhances language learning and deepens understanding. Drama-literature offers an instructional process where students are able to become members of the world communities. The drama-literature activities help connect students to develop a sensitivity to and awareness of the diversity of languages and their representative communities. Additionally, children who come to school from a non-English background need opportunities to develop communities where they can expand proficiencies in their first language (Standards for Foreign Language Learning, 1993).

Second Language Lesson 5

Between Two Worlds (Ransom, 1994) is the story of Sarah Winnemucca. This piece of historical fiction is based on the true story of Sarah as she travels between her Paiute Indian community and a community of white settlers.

Instructional Session

I. Topic: Participation in multilingual communities

II. Issues of Exploration

- Use of second languages within a larger community setting
- Using aspects of a language for personal enjoyment and enrichment
- Nonverbal language within a community and culture

III. Focusing Question: How does nonverbal communication factor into learning a second language and help establish a sense of community?

IV. Planning

- After reading *Between Two Worlds,* students select moments from the text that depict Sarah performing a ritual or task that is from her native community, as well as rituals or tasks that she performs within her new community in order to try and fit in.
- Brainstorm two lists on the blackboard with both types of rituals and tasks.
- Divide students into small groups for the purpose of creating improvised nonverbal scenes depicting Sarah performing both types of rituals or tasks. Each group should develop at least one nonverbal scene for each of the two types of rituals and tasks generated above.

V. Playing: Small groups share their nonverbal second language scenes with one another.

VI. Evaluation and Follow-Up

- Assign each student the task of thinking of a scene in which they ask someone for something they really want.
- Divide the class into pairs and instruct them to ask their partner for what they want with no words and using only physical communication.
- Discuss as a group the importance of nonverbal communication in the learning of a second language. How can the use of nonverbal communication help one fit into a community? How does nonverbal communication help you communicate within your own community?

Concluding Thoughts

The five Cs of second language learning—communication, cultures, connections, comparisons, and communities—are the critical elements of curriculum that will enable students of language to participate in multilingual contexts in culturally appropriate ways. These five Cs could also be identified as the five Cs of drama-literature learning. At their very root, interesting dramatic action and well-written literature involve audiences or participants in a good story that expresses (communicates) meaningful ideas and thoughts about a specific group of people (culture) in a unique setting (community) where conflict occurs. This conflict or struggle between persons will involve interactions (both connections and comparisons) that result in a plausible outcome. One hopes that the outcome fosters learning for both the participants and the audience. The same is true for the second language classroom where drama-literature is used to bridge content with our lives and the world in which we live.

References

Eisner, Elliot. 1979. *The Education Imagination: On the Design and Evaluation of School Programs.* New York: Macmillan.

Language Coalition. 1993. *The Standards for Foreign Language Learning: Preparing for the 21st Century.* American Council on the Teaching of

Foreign Languages, Yonkers, NY: American Council on the Teaching of Foreign Languages.

Hirschfelder, Arlene, and Beverly R. Singer. 1992. *Rising Voices: Writings of Young Native Americans.* New York: Ballantine Books.

Lowell, Susan. 1992. *The Three Little Javelinas.* Flagstaff, AZ: Northland Press.

O'Neil, Cecily, and Alan Lambert. 1982. *Drama Structure: A Practical Handbook for Teachers.* London: Hutchinson.

Paulson, Gary. 1993. *Hermanas: Sisters.* New York: Harcourt Brace Jovanovich.

Ransom, C. F. 1994. *Between Two Worlds.* New York: Scholastic.

Siks, Geraldine. 1983. *Drama with Children.* 2d ed. New York: Harper and Row.

Smith, J. Lea, and J. Daniel Herring. 1993. *Using Drama in the Classroom.* Kalamazoo, MI: Reading Horizons.

Soto, Gary. 1993. *Local News.* New York: Scholastic.

Velasquez, Gloria L. 1997. *I Used to Be a Superwoman: Superwoman Chicana.* Houston: Arte Publico Press.

10
Our Final Words

Our goal in this book is to show the role drama and literature can play in the learning cycle of education. The use of drama-literature as an instructional design to study content has extensive potential. Drama-literature encourages students to engage in independent, spontaneous, and reflective thinking. If students are to extend their thinking, then instruction has to be structured in ways that will offer opportunities for students to reflect on their thinking within a context of issues and problems unique to the academic disciplines.

We, as both drama and literature teachers, began to experiment with our respective disciplines in combination with the other. In this process of playing with the possibilities of combining drama and literature as a way to learn and as a way to know, we discovered an unlimited perspective of making content instruction firsthand and alive. Our studies of how drama-literature can open the doors to learning led us to a belief in the power of drama-literature instruction unleashing for all students the ability to use symbolic thought and language as the basis for learning by doing.

Talk—the give and take of ideas—has been the mainstay of our study of how to incorporate drama-literature as a natural way to study issues and topics. This talk will best capture our beliefs about the energy drama-literature will bring to a classroom learning setting.

Reflecting on Our Process

J. LEA: What does drama have to offer teachers as a way to teach?

J. DANIEL: Drama gives teachers an instructional tool that is developmentally appropriate for student learning. The processes of drama—moving, speaking, socializing, and decision making—encourage the development of a student's self-esteem that is pivotal to academic, social, and psychological well-being.

J. DANIEL: Why would you integrate literature into the drama rather than just doing the drama activities?

J. LEA: Literature is the human story. Drama built on literature creates natural episodes for students to find understanding of content ideas through story interpretation.

J. DANIEL: What were the first bits of knowledge you used to begin to blend drama into your literature studies?

J. LEA: The most important variable was my willingness to use drama as a way to study literature. Then, I had to begin to experiment with how to create dramatic action within the context of a story while facilitating students' participation in the dramatic action. Last but not least, I had to encourage students to reflect and to evaluate their dramatic interpretations.

J. LEA: Drama has its own inherent excitement, but what does drama provide a learner beyond the fun activity?

J. DANIEL: When a teacher incorporates drama into a learning situation, students have many chances to consider the human condition. They are given the skills to better comprehend their reality in this big, diverse world of ours.

J. DANIEL: When you work with drama in a classroom, do you typically use a holistic or a linear approach?

J. LEA: Initially my comfort level led me to use a linear approach more often. This technique would allow me to plan, before the playing, what most likely would develop. Also, I was able to act as a side-coach to encourage the dramatic action.

J. DANIEL: I really enjoy using a holistic approach when I want to get dramatic action started immediately. I also enjoy playing a character in-role with my students to keep the action flowing and help maintain concentration for the students.

J. LEA: What is the difference between story dramatization and creating improvisations?

J. DANIEL: The difference is the students' perspective. In story dramatization, students are able to live the literature by walking in the shoes of the characters, allowing them to experience a perspective other than their own. Often in conventional improvisations, the created characters are modeled after their own lives and experiences.

J. LEA: What I like best about story dramatization is the chances students have to think independently about their view of the story while working as a team player. This encourages them to play with how to create real world action.

J. DANIEL: As a language arts specialist, what hooked you on using drama in your language arts work?

J. LEA: Dramatic action in the language arts classroom initiates a setting where doing language is the mode to learn. Reading and writing the dramatic way provides students with personal connections to the mechanics and skills. By this I mean students are able to read to act, write to act, act to read, and act to write—drama lifts reading and writing off of the page through the act of demonstration.

J. DANIEL: When I began working as a drama specialist in classrooms, teachers most often asked me to tie drama to the language arts curriculum.

J. LEA: Tell me more about your drama beginnings with language arts studies.

J. DANIEL: Most teachers were interested in my work with story dramatization and how to get students to write before and after doing drama. As time passed, I began to explore the use of drama in teaching about the human condition, which was a natural fit with any social studies curriculum.

J. LEA: So how does drama fit within a social studies classroom?

J. DANIEL: Social studies becomes more than dates and facts when the students explore people, places, and times by living the curriculum through stories and dramatic action.

J. DANIEL: Other curriculum areas didn't seem to jump out at me as easily as language arts and social studies when it came to using drama as a teaching tool.

J. LEA: It seems that as we began working together and reading literature, we first played with different possibilities as to how we might integrate drama-literature into science, math, and foreign language.

J. DANIEL: It wasn't until we began to realize that to incorporate drama into content instruction, we would need to shift our goal from product knowledge to processes of learning for each discipline.

J. LEA: What I hear you saying is that drama-literature is one strategy to enliven the teaching of content information.

J. DANIEL: Right! We are not suggesting that drama-literature can teach the entire content matter, but it is an alive and fun way to teach aspects of the content.

J. DANIEL: When you think about science, what processes do you think of immediately?

J. LEA: I think about the process of inquiry—observing and gathering data to make informed conclusions.

J. DANIEL: The same process is true when drama and literature are used in the science classroom. Students read and make informed observations about the characters and events in a piece of literature, or while acting out an improvisation experiment with how someone might respond to a specific situation. Essentially inquiry is automatic.

J. DANIEL: Now, the thought of drama in the math classroom always seemed to scare me the most.

J. LEA: Because math is basically about problem solving, I could see how literature and drama could be woven into the curriculum. For instance, problem solving, communication, and reasoning are skills that are fundamental to envisioning a piece of literature.

J. DANIEL: And the same is true for a group of students involved in acting out a scene in which there is not enough food for all the characters, and a system for distributing rations must be implemented.

J. LEA: When I first thought of literature in the second language classroom, I could readily see how the reading of multicultural literature fit nicely, but the drama component seemed harder to grasp in another language.

J. DANIEL: Yes, I agree. However, since drama at its core is about communication involving groups of people, interacting by using another language or culture is really only a simple technicality in the second language classroom.

J. LEA: The second language component with drama-literature is an added dimension of our diverse world.

Drama-literature offers learners a setting to create a textual world where they shape themselves to the perspectives of the story while restructuring the story (dramatic action) with both a personal perspective and a character's perspective (Bruner, 1986). Bakhtin (1986) suggests that an inventive understanding of a story occurs when learners travel through a character or situation as deeply as possible, while keeping sight of their personal experience.

Learners, during the journey, create new meanings through dramatic action to achieve dialogue among the author of the story, other classmates, the teacher, and themselves.

Drama-literature, as a way to learn, give students institutional license to make their own decisions while using multiple sources of knowledge, particularly themselves and each other to consider problems in story interpretation. Students in a drama-literature classroom learn to act and act to learn— reading, talking, and moving through space to express their understanding of a storybook and of their own world. Our drama-literature approach to learning is a familiar and comfortable way for students to express their understanding of a story while using their imagination. Drama-literature creates a learning environment, in all content disciplines, where students experience and play with ideas rather than just memorize information to give back on a text as proof of their learning. Drama-literature embraces multifaceted ways to know and to express knowledge. It is when we widen our vision of how to teach and how students demonstrate their knowing, students will begin to create a community of learners where all students have the freedom to learn by doing. There are multiple ways to learn and multiple ways to express learning. Turner (1982) suggests the storybook author "may invent plots, situations, characters, scenery; but imaginative truth underlies surface fiction." (p. 33) This is true for students engaging in drama-literature as a way to learn. They must be able to interpret the story while they reinterpret through dramatic action.

We encourage you to attempt the integration of drama-literature into your teaching. It is through your willingness to consider the possibilities that your students will learn. And, we say, "Make our book yours!"

References

Bakhtin, M[ikhail] M. 1986. *Speech Genres and Other Late Essays.* C. Emerson and M. M. Holquist (Eds.). Austin, TX: University of Texas Press.

Bruner, Jerome. 1986. *Actual Minds, Possible Worlds.* Cambridge, MA: Harvard University Press.

Turner, V. 1982. "Liminality and the Performative Genres." In F. A. Hanson (Ed.), *Studies in Symbolism and Cultural Communication.* Lawrence, KS: University of Kansas Publications in Anthropology, 25–41.

Appendix A
Points to Remember
When Leading Drama-
Literature Activities

1. Try to guide students rather than demonstrate how they should do the activity. Avoid asking students to imitate; instead, encourage them to create and invent on their own.

2. Be positive. Use words of encouragement when the students are focused on exploring various possibilities within the activities.

3. Rarely is a student wrong during these types of activities. This point of view allows the child to succeed. You should encourage students to let his or her idea grow and develop.

4. This is not a competitive situation. We want secure creative students. Look at each idea as an individual one, rather than comparing quality of work.

5. Be interested in the process and how it evolves as opposed to focusing on a product that must be created. If a product develops naturally from the process, then encourage this for the sake of the learning process and not the final product.

6. Don't be afraid to develop a control device (such as the word "freeze," or flicking the lights on and off) for your drama/literature activities. If the students are not focused, and the activities are going awry, then use the control device to stop the activity and reevaluate. You want creativity, not chaos.

Appendix B
Building Effective Groups for Drama-Literature Activities

Step 1: Getting Started
- Teacher/leader needs to explain to the students what they can expect during the activity.
- Provide an opportunity for students to get to know you and one another.

Step 2: Creating the Environment
- Provide group-centered learning activities.
- Use various types of groupings (duet, small group, entire class).
- Arrange groups so that students can see and hear one another.
- Involve students in setting the goals for the class session/activity.
- Redirect questions to the group as opposed to always answering the questions.
- Think of yourself as an observer and a resource.
- Develop activities that cannot be accomplished without the input and work of several group members.
- Allow for consensus to be the guiding force for decision making.

Step 3: Dealing with Conflict
- Approach conflict with active listening.
- Try not to dictate.
- Use the group's feelings to help discover solutions.

Step 4: Reaching an Outcome

- Create and maintain a clear focus for the group.
- Allow for setbacks to occur.
- Provide a balance for the group to work on the outcome of the activity as well as group dynamics.

Step 5: Wrapping It Up

- Inform the group that the experience is indeed ending.
- Provide an opportunity for students to express their feelings about the experience through some type of reflection and evaluation.

For a more in-depth look at developing effective group work, read Gene Stanford, *Developing Effective Classroom Groups.* (New York: Hart, 1977).

Appendix C
Glossary of Drama Terms

Action (playable action): The physical pursuit of a specific objective in a scene. Defines what the character is doing in a scene. Without action, a scene is flat and will not work.

Actor/Player: A performer who assumes the role of a character in a play.

Characterization: How the actor/player uses his/her mind (imagination), body, and voice to create and portray a character in a play.

Conflict: The opposition of objectives, desires, or actions that creates the dramatic tension in a play.

Costume: The clothing or pieces of clothing worn by an actor to communicate information about the character they are portraying or the environment in which they live.

Critic: A specialist in the evaluation of literary and artistic theater work. This person usually works for newspapers, magazines, radio, or television.

Designer: The individual responsible for the creation of the visual or sound aspects of a theater production, including costumes, scenery, props, lights, makeup, and sound.

Dialogue: The conversational lines of the play spoken between two or more characters.

Director: The person responsible for guiding and supervising actors and designers in the creation of the play's production according to his or her interpretation/vision/concept.

Ensemble: An artistic team working together to create a unified theatrical production in accordance with the director's concept.

Expression: The physical and vocal skills used by the actor/player to convey mood, emotion, or personality of the character they are portraying.

Improvisation: The spontaneous unscripted and sometimes unrehearsed use of voice and movement to act out a specific situation. The actors in an improvisation must be able to establish through their speech and physicality who they are, where they are, and what they are doing in the spontaneous scene.

Lighting: The placement and color of light to create and communicate to an audience the environment, mood, and feeling of a play.

Makeup: Cosmetics and wigs used to visually transform an actor into a character.

Mime: An actor who conveys his/her character (who they are, where they are, and what they are doing) without using words.

Monologue: A long speech or passage from a play that is spoken by one character. The character may be addressing the audience directly, another character on stage, or sharing internal thoughts out loud to him/herself.

Motivation: The reasons why a character behaves in a certain way. The specific reasons can be related to any or all of the following—past history, present circumstances, relationships with other characters, and future goals or objectives.

Objective: The one primary action that includes all the actions a character performs from scene to scene throughout the play. It is what the character wants most of all.

Pantomime: When gesture and movement are used by the actor to convey the presence of imagined objects.

Performance: A single presentation of a theatrical event.

Playwright: The person who conceives, develops, and writes the script for the dramatic performance.

Plot: The events and the characters interaction with those events form the basis of the play's story.

Production: The final staging (including the actors and design elements) of a play for presentation to an audience.

Property (Prop): Any object that appears on stage during a performance that could be moved by the actor including furniture, dishes, books, pillows, etc.

Scenery: The environment that is created and built for the production. The setting can be created with curtains, flats, backdrops, or platforms and designed to reflect time, place, mood, or feeling.

Script/Play: The written dialogue, monologues, stage directions, and descriptions for a dramatic production.

Sound: The effects including music an audience hears during a performance to communicate character, context, mood, or environment.

Stage directions: The instructions a playwright includes in the script in order to help directors and actors understand the action of the play. Information about events in the play's environment may also be included in the stage directions.

Tableau: A staging technique used to freeze the action of a scene in play. A frozen picture for the audience to view, often used as a starting or ending point of a scene.